"Could we swim?" Damiene asked softly, longing licking through her like a flame.

"Yes," Piers said. He wanted her with an elemental need he'd known only with her, never before with anyone or anything. He could have exploded with desire, yet he wanted to cherish and care for her as though she were the most precious thing on earth. She was . . .

She started toward her room, but he tugged her back. "I thought I'd get my suit."

"You don't need one, darling."

She gasped and stared up at him. His features were silvered by the low beam of the hall light. "Devil." She raised her hand to caress his beautiful mouth, and he pressed his lips to her palm.

"I want to see you in the water," he murmured, "gaze at your creamy skin, your lovely curves." He paused, then added, "What do you want?"

Damiene's turquoise eyes shone with the fires of passion. "I want you . . ."

WHAT ARE *LOVESWEPT* ROMANCES?

They are stories of true romance and touching emotion. We believe those two very important ingredients are constants in our highly sensual and very believable stories in the *LOVESWEPT* line. Our goal is to give you, the reader, stories of consistently high quality that may sometimes make you laugh, sometimes make you cry, but are always fresh and creative and contain many delightful surprises within their pages.

Most romance fans read an enormous number of books. Those they truly love, they keep. Others may be traded with friends and soon forgotten. We hope that each *LOVESWEPT* romance will be a treasure—a "keeper." We will always try to publish

LOVE STORIES YOU'LL NEVER FORGET
BY AUTHORS YOU'LL ALWAYS REMEMBER

The Editors

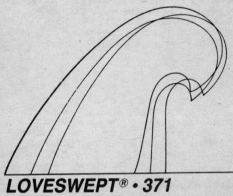

LOVESWEPT® • 371

Helen Mittermeyer
Men of Ice:
Quicksilver

 BANTAM BOOKS
NEW YORK • TORONTO • LONDON • SYDNEY • AUCKLAND

QUICKSILVER

A Bantam Book / December 1989

If you would be interested in receiving protective vinyl
covers for your Loveswept books, please write to this address
for information:

Loveswept
Bantam Books
P.O. Box 985
Hicksville, NY 11802

ISBN 0-553-22043-8

Published simultaneously in the United States and Canada

Bantam Books are published by Bantam Books, a division
of Bantam Doubleday Dell Publishing Group, Inc. Its trademark, consisting of the words "Bantam Books" and the
portrayal of a rooster, is Registered in U.S. Patent and
Trademark Office and in other countries. Marca Registrada.
Bantam Books, 666 Fifth Avenue, New York, New York 10103.

PRINTED IN THE UNITED STATES OF AMERICA

O   0 9 8 7 6 5 4 3 2 1

One
***

Early spring was just around the corner. Snow still
fell in northern Nevada, but here, in Las Vegas, it
was balmy. Piers Larraby strolled through the parking lot toward the street. He was in no hurry to
reach the casino. Lately, the endless round of gambling was getting to him. Though there was still a
measure of excitement, the luster had faded.

It was time he got back to his business full-time,
he thought. The information he'd stumbled on three
months before about Berto's death hadn't led to anything concrete. So he'd go back to being actively
involved in his real estate and casino interests until
he got another lead. Sometimes it seemed so fruitless, but he had no intention of giving up the search.
He'd damn well find who burned the London club
and killed his partner two years earlier.

A sense of futility suddenly filled him, and he
decided to stay in Las Vegas only for another week.
After the cocktail party he had planned, he would

return to New York, or maybe Monaco, and hope that there—

His thoughts were shattered instantly as he turned the corner onto the street. A woman was running toward him, panic on her face. A car was following her, dogging her every step. Although the vehicle wasn't speeding, it came on inexorably, following her onto the sidewalk. The windows were tinted black, so it seemed the car had a life of its own.

Before he thought of the consequences, Piers was racing to her. The image of what might happen spurred him to greater speed. Just as the car reached her, he swept her into his arms.

The car barely missed them as he sailed over some decorative cacti in front of a casino, the woman clenched tightly to him. Then the car was past and they landed in a heap on the soft ground.

Shock held Piers motionless for long moments. At last he lifted his head and stared down at a very lovely face. Even the Las Vegas neon night couldn't mask the translucence of her skin or the beauty of her eyes.

"Are you hurt?" he asked softly.

"I don't think so. Thanks."

Assisting the woman to her feet, he stared down at her, jolted more by her turquoise eyes than the uproar behind them. "Are you sure you're all right?"

She studied him warily, then put a hand to her face. "I think I lost my glasses," she said. "Could you help me find them?"

"I'll try." He knelt down, searching the earth around him, feeling gingerly among the cacti. Nothing. He straightened. "Sorry, I don't . . ." But he was talking to air. The woman with turquoise eyes had vanished.

Brushing himself off, he vaulted over the cacti again and looked up and down the street. Hordes of people were gathering, converging on a security officer and two policemen. There was no one who even resembled the woman with silvery blonde hair. She'd been tall, and sweetly muscled by the feel of her, curved delicately but strongly. Had she been a figment of his imagination?

"Excuse me, sir." One of the policeman had approached him, and was looking at him closely. "Witnesses have said that the car seemed to be out of control and almost hit a woman. Did you see anything?"

"Not really. I went for cover when I saw the car on the sidewalk," Piers said casually. There wasn't much he could tell the police anyway, so he kept to himself his suspicion that the driver of the car had been deliberately trying to run the woman down. "If you'll excuse me. Good evening, Officer."

Ignoring the man's assessing look, Piers turned to the casino behind him. He glanced up and down the street once more, looking for the beautiful, mysterious woman, then entered Vince's. He generally spent a good share of his time there when he was in Vegas. Vince Dalrymple was Berto's brother, and there was a bond between Piers and Vince because of that.

Piers entered the main gambling area of the casino, nodding to several people he knew. As he strode through the crowded noisy main room, heading for the baccarat table, he glanced around, wariness an integral part of him. When his gaze fixed on the roulette table, everything else left his mind.

He moved back to a wall and leaned against it,

watching his lady of the night, the lady with the turquoise eyes. She was now absorbed in a roulette game, pushing the supposedly lost glasses up her nose with one finger. Even in the garish light of the casino she had a haunting otherworldly quality. Gorgeous and gamine. Svelte and simple. Who was she?

He'd seen more beautiful women, many of them. But he'd never before seen such an amalgam of sophistication and naïveté, elegance and sweetness. In addition, her strange behavior pricked at him. Why had she run away from him? How could she sit there and calmly play roulette after nearly being hit by a car?

Annoyed that the woman so effortlessly captivated him, he turned away. As he strode to the baccarat table, he consciously put the woman out of his mind. There were ways to find out about her, and he would. Vince usually knew his clientele.

As if his thoughts had conjured up the man, he saw Vince walking toward him. As always, he felt the familiar pang of loss. Tall and broadly built, with dark hair, dark eyes, and a wide smile, Vince looked remarkably like his brother Berto.

"Good evening, Piers," Vince said in his cultured British accent.

"Vince, how are you? I feel lucky."

Vince rolled his eyes. "That's how you got the name Quicksilver. I've never seen anyone lift the silver from casino coffers so fast. You don't lose often, friend, luck or no." Vince grimaced as Piers laughed. "I would return to the club in London if you promised not to frequent the place."

Piers grinned. He'd broken a bank or two in Vince's London casino. "I'm playing only baccarat tonight,

Vince," he said, continuing on to the table. "I shouldn't win more than a few thousand."

Vince laughed and waved him away. Piers reached the table and took one last look at the blonde. He fully intended to get some answers from her.

Two hours later Piers rose from the table, sweeping an impressive number of chips into his hands. As he walked toward the cashier, Vince approached him, frowning.

"Going to throw me out?" Piers asked languidly.

"I should. By the exasperated looks at your table, you managed to put some holes in our budget." He took Piers's arm and moved him off to a relatively quiet corner. "How are things going?"

"About the same." Piers didn't pretend to misunderstand. Vince was well aware of his search for Berto's killer.

"Don't tense up, Piers. We'll get them." Piers smiled, but Vince wasn't fooled. "I don't like that look."

Piers shrugged. "I still get angry when I think about Berto."

"I know what you mean," Vince said tightly.

Piers nodded. When one of the pit bosses motioned to Vince, Piers moved away. His gaze swept the crowded room as he strode through it, and he realized he was looking for the blonde. He finally glimpsed her at a blackjack table, a small but respectable stack of chips by her elbow. He watched her for a few minutes, and when the man beside her gathered his chips and left, Piers took his place.

The woman edged up her facedown card and glanced at it, and he took the opportunity to study her more closely. She wasn't as young as he'd first thought, but was probably in her late twenties. A fresh scrape on her arm showed below the short sleeve of her dress. Had she gotten that when they'd landed behind the cacti? There was a mark on her chin as well.

Her skin was luminescent with a rosy hue that owed little to makeup. Her light brown brows arched over eyes that had a slightly Asian look to them. Her silver-blonde hair was twisted at her neck in a chignon. He wondered if it was long enough to twist around his own neck if they made love. Her dress wasn't haute couture, but it had been well chosen and suited her. A career woman on vacation? Or a discreet woman of the streets? Professional gambler? Or a housewife out for an evening? Since the picture of her with husband and children didn't sit well, he discarded the last. He was still staring at her, wondering about her, when she glanced up at him.

"Are you going to stare," Damiene Belson asked, "or do you want to play this hand? The dealer's waiting."

At first she hadn't noticed the man who'd sat down next to her. She'd been intently listening to the conversation of the two men on her other side. But the prolonged pause had made her glance at the newcomer, then she'd taken a longer look at him. Was he the one who'd saved her from the car? She shivered at the memory. She'd almost been killed!

Cold perspiration beaded her upper lip as she risked another look at him. He was tall and sleekly muscled, expensively dressed in a raw silk jacket and crisp linen slacks. And his smile. It was as sweetly deceptive as Satan's own. A tall, tanned, dangerous man with bourbon-colored eyes. He'd saved her life. She was sure of that now, and she was grateful. But she had to be cautious too. There were so many types of hangers-on in casinos. It hadn't taken long to discover that. What was he? A gambler, gigolo, or gangster? Or enemy? Another shiver coursed over her as her gaze locked with his.

"They're an even deeper turquoise than I first thought," he murmured.

"What?" she asked, confused.

He didn't answer. He glanced at the dealer and said, "I'm in."

As they played, Piers found himself having difficulty concentrating on the cards for the first time ever. Though he won steadily, he kept being distracted by the woman beside him. He admired her long, graceful fingers as she checked her cards . . . and wondered how it would feel to have those slender hands slide over his naked skin. The sound of her husky voice seemed to shimmer over him . . . and he wanted to hear her cry out his name in passion. His fascination with her baffled him and angered him, yet he wouldn't walk away from her even if someone held a gun to his head. Not, at least, until he learned her name.

She didn't look at him again as they played, and it was well past midnight when she finally rose from the table. He stood at the same time and gathered his chips.

He followed her to the cash window, then hurried after her when he saw her leave the casino. Her body seemed to float, her long legs striding strongly and smoothly. A familiar fire simmered in his lower body. The breathlessness and need to cherish that accompanied it were new sensations.

Stepping outside, he waved away the doorman who approached the woman. "May I offer you a ride?"

She glanced at him. "No," she said, and walked away from him, down toward the street.

"I'll walk with you, then," he said, catching up with her. "It can be dangerous to walk by yourself at this late hour. A car could come by and hit you." He noted how she stiffened, how her gaze flashed left and right.

"But the danger might be you." She stopped, then headed back to the doorman. "Better call me a cab," she said to him.

"Ah, very well, miss. But I thought you were with Mr. Larraby."

She turned to look at Piers. "That's you."

He nodded. Her beautiful hands flexed and un- flexed, her tall, lissome body poised as though for flight. He knew he'd chase her if she ran. Hell! What was the matter with him?

"They seem to know you here," she said hesitantly.

"I can get you a reference from Vincent Dalrymple."

"I don't know him. For all I know, he could be the Las Vegas Strangler and you could be his sidekick, Tonto."

"That's the Lone Ranger."

"Whatever."

Damiene allowed her body to relax a little. He wasn't just good-looking, he was scintillating. As he stood there watching her, he made her think of a leashed tiger, its awesome power barely restrained. And his lazy smile was like a laser, peeling away her de- fenses, seeing through her.

She shook her head. The strain of being on the road, of worrying about her finances and clearing her brother's name, was getting to her. Just one night without concern and fear, with uninterrupted, dreamless sleep, would be heaven. That dive over the cacti hadn't helped. Her left arm was still tender, and there was a rawness on her chin.

"I believe you've shocked John," the man called Larraby said. "You think Mr. Dalrymple is a good man, don't you, John?"

"I certainly do," the doorman replied. "He's good to his employees. Pay raises come along regular as clockwork."

The man's lofty tone touched Damiene, but her guard was still up. "Fine," she said tartly, "and I don't know any of you. Better get me a cab."

"I'll try, miss."

"Take a chance with me," the other man said. "I'll take you straight home."

His eyes were like lightning on a hot summer night, setting off fires inside her. She told herself a blistering reply was the only way to handle this. "All right," she said. "But straight to my motel."

Was she out of her mind? she asked herself. During the past six weeks she'd fine-honed survival instincts she hadn't even known she had. Those instincts had carried her, relatively unscathed, from Atlantic City to Las Vegas. It was foolhardy to relax her vigilance when she might be getting close to her quarry. But she remembered the sensation of this man sweeping her into his arms and leaping over the cacti to save her life. She had felt safe then.

When she wheeled around to accompany him to the car park, Piers's gaze was caught by the expanse of slender sleek leg that showed beneath her flaring skirt. His libido heated at the thought of those sinuous limbs wrapping around his body. They reached his car and he touched her arm. "Here we are."

She stared at the Lamborghini. "Nice car. Do you steal for a living?"

"Only now and then."

"That must be a comfort to your friends."

When he closed the door on her, Damiene felt cocooned . . . trapped. Had she been foolish? In the list of the five most stupid things to do, getting in a car with a stranger had to be right at the top. What was the matter with her? For a moment she wanted to leap from the car and run, and keep on running. It would have been almost comforting to identify the emotion as fear. But fear wasn't what she felt when she looked at him. As he settled behind the wheel, she turned to him. "I'm staying at the El Dorado. You might not know it."

"Direct me."

The powerful car roared to life, and he careened out of the car park. He could hear the wariness still in her voice and had a sudden need to reassure her. This woman had a peculiar yet unshakable effect on him.

"Do you collect speeding tickets?" she asked.

"Rarely get them. Did you know the driver of the car that tried to run you down earlier?" His hands tightened on the wheel as he recalled the chase.

"Of course not," she said, her voice trembling slightly. She cleared her throat. "I probably just got in the way. Maybe it was a gang trying to get into the casino safe."

"No doubt. I'm sure there are many instances of cars crashing into banks and casinos and making off with the loot."

"There's no need to be sarcastic."

"True. Just as there's no need for you to assume I'm a fool."

They drove for a distance in silence.

Damiene felt absurdly safe.

A quiet excitement coursed through Piers.

"My name is Piers Larraby," he said suddenly. Reaching out, he clasped her hand. A shocking red-hot charge exploded within him.

"I'm—I'm Damiene Belson." Spotting the gold-nugget sign of her motel, she exhaled in relief. She had to get away from Piers Larraby. That sense of security could be dangerous. Still, she was disappointed when he released her.

Piers pulled up and stopped the car, his gaze going over the two-story second-rate motel. "Will you let me take you out to supper?" He didn't want to say good-bye to Damiene Belson. He wanted more of her warmth, her tartness and sweetness.

"No. I'm very tired."

"How about lunch tomorrow . . ." His voice trailed off as he realized she wasn't listening. His gaze followed hers. Two men were moving slowly along the motel's upper balcony, checking door numbers.

"Ah, about that supper," Damiene said, trying to keep the fear from her voice. Getting away from the motel was paramount. "I guess I could use some food. Could we go now?" How had they found her so soon? She'd been so careful.

Piers watched the men stop in front of a door, knock twice, then insert what could have been a key into the lock. "Your place?" He knew she wasn't aware that her fingers were digging into his arm. He put his hand over hers.

"Yes. Crime is on the rise." She didn't look at him. "Maybe you could let me off somewhere downtown."

"I could do that, but let me make a call first."

He saw her stiffen, her free hand edging toward the car door latch. "I'm not your enemy," he said quickly. He lifted her hand to his mouth, kissing it lightly.

"No?" Her fingers curled around his hand.

"No. But you might want your things taken out of there before the place gets trashed. They might be house dicks, but they don't look like it to me." Perversely, he was glad the men were there. It gave him a chance to keep her safe and with him.

"Me either," she mumbled.

"I have a friend who'll get your things for you, then we can relax over some good food." He peeled out of the parking lot, then dialed a number on the cellular phone. "Vince? Get someone over to the El Dorado Motel. There are a couple of heavies over there. Bent on ransacking, I suppose. It's room number . . ." He glanced at Damiene.

"Two two seven." She rubbed her hands together, trying to dry the cold sweat on her palms. Why hadn't he called the police? He hadn't even asked her if she wanted them called.

"Get all the belongings, Vince, and take them to my place. Yes, you heard right. Better hurry . . . and be careful. They're big. No, I don't care if they get bruised a little. Watch yourself. Thanks." Piers replaced the phone and made a left turn off the Strip.

Damiene exhaled shakily. "This isn't the way downtown."

"No. We're going to my place. We'll have supper there."

"And if I don't want to accompany you, Piers Larraby?" He was too damned good-looking and self-assured for his own good. A definite pirate type. His black hair was silvered at the temples, and his face was like sculpted granite, with a square chin and high-planed cheeks.

"Then I'll bring you back to the center of Las Vegas," he said. Frazzled as she might be, her regal air would have done justice to Queen Victoria. And she looked even more gorgeous without her glasses on, if that was possible. "Do you always wear glasses?"

"Rarely. But my eyes have been tired lately." Too many casinos, too many late nights.

"I'll make sure you get an early night."

"And I can count on that?" It would be so simple to take the path of least resistance for once, Damiene thought. What was there about Piers Larraby that made her want to take a chance on him? Perhaps it was just fear and lack of sleep that were making her do crazy things.

"You're impugning my honor, lady."

"The honor of a gambler?"

"There is such a thing." He had a feeling she had cultivated her sharp tongue in self-defense. But who did she need protection from? "Shall we start again?"

Like a balloon pierced by a pin, she sagged back in her seat. "Maybe it would be better if we forgot this conversation and the—"

"Wait, Damiene, don't say any more. Let's get some supper and relax. Then we'll talk about the next step. Fair enough?"

She nodded, facing him. "They call you Quicksilver, don't they? It took me a little while to connect you with the name Piers Larraby."

"Some people call me that," he said shortly.

"Then I think I might."

His head snapped toward her. She smiled imp- ishly, and a dimple appeared at a corner of her mouth. The car veered under his hands. Who was Damiene Belson? Gamine or goddess?

"What's wrong with the car?" she asked.

"Nothing." Her teasing smile had sent his libido into a throbbing ascension. She was incredibly sen- sual, yet in a natural, unaffected way. She intrigued him, stung him into life.

From his peripheral vision he saw her rest her head against the seat. In minutes, he could tell from her slowed breathing that she was asleep. A surge of protectiveness filled him. He glanced at her again as he drove off the expressway onto a two-lane high- way. In less than a mile he was driving through a gate and up a curving knoll to the adobe house that sat on its crest. Though it was relatively close to the city, the house was private, well screened by brush and cacti from the highway. The back opened onto the desert.

Piers had bought it, after Berto's death. He had needed a place in Las Vegas for whenever he fol- lowed leads there. Vince had told him about it, and he'd known at once it was a rare find. It had more than paid for itself because of its privacy. Only a few people knew about it. He hid out there when the world closed in on him. Though he had a place in the hills above Monaco, an apartment in Manhat- tan, and a flat in London, Las Vegas was home.

He stopped the car in front of the sprawling one- story building, its sand color melding with the desert behind it. Colorful cacti surrounded the house, and the coral shutters complemented it.

He turned in his seat and looked at the too-slender woman next to him. Common sense told him he was foolish to have invited her to his sanctum. She seemed to be on the run. Had he brought a thief to his home?

He went around to the passenger side and opened the door. Leaning over her, he gave in to the irresistible impulse and kissed her gently. "Wake up, we're home."

Her eyes fluttered open. At first she smiled widely, then her expression became tentative and wary. "Home? I haven't heard that word in a while." She blinked, coming fully awake. "Sorry. I didn't mean to sack out on you."

He reached in and lifted her from the car. "Been keeping too tight a schedule?" As he made his way up the crushed-stone drive, he searched her face. Fatigue was there along with an almost hidden trepidation.

"Burning the candle at both ends, as they say." This was crazy, she thought. A complete stranger was carrying her toward his house and all she could think about was dinner. "You said something about food."

"So I did."

The door was opened before they reached it.

"Miguel, this is Miss Belson," Piers said, setting her down. "Damiene, this is Miguel." He leaned toward her and murmured, "You're staring."

"I've never seen a Mexican sumo wrestler," she muttered. "Hello, Miguel." The greeting grunted in return may have been friendly or not. "Maybe I'd better go back to Las Vegas."

"Nonsense, Miguel took an instant liking to you, didn't you, Miguel?"

Again the sound came from Miguel, a cross between a porcine snort and a canine whuff.

"He did?" she said. "My, you are a past master at hiding your glee, aren't you, Miguel?"

Miguel looked at her unblinkingly.

"Miss Belson is our guest for dinner." Piers took hold of her upper arm and whisked her into the house.

"Hey, wait a minute," she exclaimed, struggling to free herself. "Why are you—ohh, isn't this beautiful."

Piers had led her down a wide, tiled corridor to a room at the back of the house. With glass walls on three sides, it seemed to be an extension of the desert itself. She sighed, gazing around her. All manner of succulents were hanging and standing in front of the windows in lieu of drapes. The room was spacious, designed to catch the daylight, allowing it to reflect off the indoor pool at the far end.

"This place is huge," she said.

"I had it custom built. We can eat out here if you like, and watch the desert lights."

"Sounds wonderful." Her stomach growled.

"You are hungry." Piers went to a wall speaker and pressed the button, mumbling something rapidly in Spanish.

"Your accent is pure Castilian," Damiene remarked when he faced her again.

"And you recognized that? Have you been to Spain?" He had an urge to know everything about her.

"Yes." She didn't want to discuss the year she had studied in Spain. It would evoke painful memories of her brother Gilbert coming to visit her.

Her sudden restraint made Piers wonder what she was hiding. "Do you like Spain?"

"Yes." Turning her back, Damiene walked to the edge of the pool, effectively cutting off the conversation.

"Would you like to swim?" he asked.

"Not right now." She stiffened, sensing him at her back.

"You have beautiful hair, Damiene Belson," he said. Leaning close, he inhaled her fragrance, then nuzzled his face in the thick chignon at the base of her neck. "It must be long when it's loose."

"Thank you, it is." The heat from his body seemed to penetrate hers. Instead of putting her on her guard, his nearness relaxed her.

She had felt a chill since she'd seen the men enter her motel room. Now Quicksilver's presence was melting away that chill.

His strong arms slid around her waist. "You're a little too thin for your height." Her body was silkily curved with muscle, and wonderfully sensual.

"No doubt your vast experience with women makes you think so." Why did that thought sting her?

"Getting testy?" He nipped her earlobe. She was tart and saucy . . . and adorable. If he were smart, he'd drive her back to Las Vegas and leave her there. There was no room in his life for a Damiene Belson.

Damiene cleared her throat and tried to move away from him. The man had enough sexual power to blow the lights of the city and restart them.

Hearing a noise behind them, Piers turned. "Ah, Miguel, just in time." With one arm around her, he led her to the table, where Miguel was spreading out food. "Here we are, jalapeño cheese dip."

"That will scald my insides."

Piers dipped a cracker into it, shaking his head. "This is mild. Taste."

"Ummm, I like it." She sank into the chair he held for her, her mouth watering at the display of the finger food. "Grapes, I love them. And melon."

Had it been long since she'd eaten, Piers wondered. She'd certainly made enough money to buy a decent meal. He sat down opposite her, watching her. As eagerly as she ate, he was surprised at the expressions of sadness and worry that crossed her lovely, delicate face. What was she thinking? Why was she here in Las Vegas, apparently in trouble? It shocked him how much he wanted to know her thoughts, her feelings.

"Do you have a system when you gamble?" he asked abruptly.

Her wariness returned. "Sometimes I watch until I see a table where no one has won in a while and I sit there."

"That's your system?"

"I didn't say I had one, you did."

"True." She was evasive, cautious. Damiene Belson was intriguing him more and more. Should he probe? He had a mission of his own to pursue. But he couldn't stem the flood of curiosity about the sophisticated gamine who sat across the table from him enjoying her food as though she'd missed a string of meals. "Don't spoil your supper," he told her lightly.

"Not a chance." She paused. "You're not eating. And I'm taking everything." A blush climbed up her neck. She pushed a tray of frijitas toward him as though they might attack her at any moment.

"It's all right. Eat. I'm not hungry." He rose and walked around the table to her. "I wasn't taking a shot. Trust me?"

When his hands caressed her shoulder, she felt a sudden dizziness. "Yes, but I *was* hogging the food."

"You were savoring what was put in front of you." He dragged up a chair so that he could sit close to her. Their knees touched. "You can even feed me if you think I'm not getting enough." His mouth went dry at the thought of her doing that.

"I don't think that," she said. "You're built like an athlete, tall, muscular, sexy . . ." Her words died as she listened to herself.

Piers watched the blush creep up her neck again, stunned at how much her words affected him. He'd been flattered by plenty of women. But Damiene's words delighted him, seeming genuine and unaffected. He leaned forward and kissed her, his lips lingering. "Thank you for those kind words."

"I've been known to chatter." His smile ran over her like a caress. It took all she had to stem the shudder that threatened her.

"Oh, please," he said, "don't call the words back."

His roguish look made her smile.

He stroked a finger across her lips. "You have a wonderful smile." Touching her lifted his spirit, fired his blood.

"Thank you."

He took her hand and kissed her again, his mouth feathering against her lips.

Neither heard the door open, or the padding of sandals across the tiles.

"Vince's at the door . . . with stuff."

Damiene jerked away from Piers, looking everywhere but at the outsized houseman.

"Miguel, your timing was excellent."

"Angry, are you? Then I tell Vince to disappear?"

"No, dammit. Wait. I'll see him in the living room." Piers turned back to Damiene and kissed her cheek. "I think this will be your things. Eat and I'll be back. Look at me."

She looked up, her smile tentative.

"Miss me a little." He kissed her once more, then rose and strode from the room.

Piers found Vince standing next to a few pieces of mismatched luggage.

"Hi," Vince said. "She didn't have many bags—I packed the stuff myself, so I know it's a woman. We tangled with the guys at her place, but they got away." Vince's craggy face tightened. "Those were serious, bad dudes. Who is this lady? And who hates her?"

Two

Had she really been at his house for three days, Damiene wondered as she changed into her bathing suit for an afternoon swim. Though her determination to find her brother's killer hadn't weakened, her anxiety had lessened. That was almost euphoric. She felt safe . . . and comforted. Piers Larraby had done that.

She hadn't intended to stay at his house, and certainly not for more than one night. That first day, though, she'd slept around the clock, not rising until the middle of the afternoon. The exhaustion from six weeks of searching coupled with delayed reaction to the car attack and the men breaking into her motel room had taken their toll. When she'd finally seen Piers at dinner, he had convinced her there was no sense in her leaving that night.

She woke up the next morning determined to insist that he drive her back to Las Vegas. But as she ate her breakfast, Miguel told her Piers was busy that morning and wouldn't be free until lunch. Almost relieved at the reprieve, she took advantage of the indoor pool, then relaxed in the hot tub.

Part of her was uneasy at this inactivity, demanding that she return to Vegas and start making her rounds of the casinos again, hoping to hear the slightest clue about her brother's murderer. But the rest of her succumbed to the delights of Piers's home. And, she admitted, to Piers himself.

He spent that afternoon with her, taking a walk through the desert with her and telling her fascinating stories about some of the high rollers and celebrities he'd gambled with in exclusive clubs in Europe. Then subtly he tried to learn more about her. As relaxed as she was with him, though, she was still on her guard, and easily turned his questions aside.

She couldn't so easily turn aside the sensual awareness she felt when she was with him. He didn't kiss her again, yet he didn't miss an opportunity to touch her, smoothing her hair back from her face, taking her hand to show her something, brushing his fingers across her shoulders when he seated her at dinner. She shivered every time his gaze settled on her, and she wondered why she even bothered wearing clothes. He seemed able to see right through them.

They stayed up late that night, talking and dancing in the big glass-walled room. Her caution and reserve seeped away a little more with each passing moment. She was inexplicably and irresistibly drawn to him, and there was so much she longed to tell him about herself. From the mundane—that she was a CPA and ran a small accounting firm with a partner—to the secrets of her heart—that when the wild geese flew over her family's lakeside cottage, their calls drowning out speech, she longed to rise with them.

As he held her in his arms, their bodies brushing lightly and barely swaying in rhythm to a soft melody, she realized she had met a wonderful man at the worst possible time. She was determined to continue her quest for Gilbert's killer, even at the risk of her own life. But she wouldn't risk Piers's life. She knew she couldn't tell him about her brother . . . and she couldn't stay with him. If something happened to him because of her . . .

He had left her at her bedroom door with the most chaste of kisses. Now, as Damiene stood poised on the side of the pool, she hoped a vigorous workout would take the edge off the shocking sensual hunger that was gnawing inside her. No man had ever made her feel the way Piers did—and it frightened and intoxicated her.

She dove into the water, and to take her mind off the thought of his kisses, she wondered about him. This morning, like the morning before, he was in his study with the door tightly closed. Also like the morning before, an express package had been delivered, and Miguel had taken it directly to Piers. The phone rang several times over the next few hours, then Piers emerged to tell her he had to go to Las Vegas to meet with someone.

If he was simply a gambler, she mused, her arms slicing effortlessly through the water, what did he work on in the mornings? Investments for his winnings? That was possible, for it was obvious from this house, his car, and his clothes that he was quite well off. Yet she had the sense that Piers was more than a professional gambler, that there were greater depths to him. She longed to learn more about him, but knew that would mean telling him more about herself, why she was in Vegas . . .

For a moment Gilbert's face seemed to appear before her, smiling, his blue eyes alight with laughter. An aching pain gripped her as she wondered yet again why anyone would have killed her cheerful, loving brother. She forced his image and the pain aside, telling herself to forget for just a little while.

A sudden splash startled her. She stopped swimming and glanced around, treading water. Through her goggles the world looked hazy. Was it Piers? Could he be back from Las Vegas already?

His sleek dark head popped out of the water. Droplets beaded on his broad, tanned shoulders, and his eyes were gleaming. "Hi. I missed you."

"Piers!" And she had missed him. So much. Of their own volition, her hands reached for him.

He grabbed her and pressed his mouth to hers, his tongue skating across her lips.

At last! she thought, opening to him.

Her heart thudded painfully at his velvety intrusion. The world spun off its axis, tipping them into the vortex of sexual heat. Their bodies grew heavy, languorous, and they sank into the depths of the pool. It had all been too fast, too intense, too crazy, she thought. But she couldn't help herself. She needed to hold him.

When they resurfaced, they were both out of breath, and not just from lack of oxygen.

Piers felt as though his being had just been melded with her. He didn't believe in fantasies like love at first sight, but he did know that Damiene Belson had been a sweet part of his life from the moment he'd met her. That wasn't going to change.

"I—I thought—you—had a—meeting." Although her lungs had filled with oxygen, she gasped as desire swept through her like a flash flood. He was more than quicksilver, he was lightning and rockets all in one. Lord! What was she doing to herself? Didn't she have enough problems? Hadn't a near hit with a car been enough? Even now, thinking about it, she could barely quell a shudder.

"I did have a meeting," he said.

"Oh. You don't have to hold me, I can tread water."

"I like it this way."

"All right."

He pressed closer, kissing her again. God, he needed her!

"Here are the munchies, señorita, with no hot peppers."

Piers pulled back, glaring up at his houseman. "Miguel, go away."

Miguel's shrug spoke volumes. "She is always hungry. What can I do?"

"You can damn well stop popping in here every—"

"I told him I could eat something." Damiene freed herself and swam to the side of the pool, hoisting herself up. "Thank you, Miguel."

"I understand eating," Miguel said. "I do it myself."

She wasn't quite sure if his grimace was friendly or not, but she smiled anyway. "Thank you."

Pulling himself out of the pool, Piers stalked to her side, his glare following the houseman from the solarium. He wanted Damiene, wanted to keep her, care for her . . . and he didn't want interruptions.

Laughter bubbled out of her. "You look like a little boy who's been told there's no Christmas this year."

Watching her beautiful features melt in amusement did something to his insides. "I should punch him in the mouth," he said softly, his head bending toward her.

"You're fond of Miguel."

"I'll tear his ears off if he comes in again when I'm loving you." He said this against her mouth. The touch of her satiny lips against his had his heart pounding in his chest.

"We're not at the stage of loving yet," she said, willing her pulse beat back to normal.

"But we are, angel. I'm loving you with all of me, and right now with my eyes."

And he was! she thought. Her body was heating to boiling, her blood set afire by those bourbon eyes of his. "Ah, how was your meeting?"

"You're out of breath." He leaned close, his tongue touching a corner of her lips. "Could it just be from the swimming?" His tongue outlined her lips, stroked their soft insides, then retreated.

In self-defense she popped a plum into her mouth and bit down on it.

She chuckled as he scowled at her. "Did I put a crimp in your plans?" Why was she so giddy, she wondered. She should resist him and the message she read in his eyes. Had she completely lost her reason?

"Yes," he said. His gaze flickered over her, admiring her tall, sleek body in the white racing suit. She was a magnificent woman, inside and out, and he had felt more alive in these past three days than in the previous two years.

Why did she have so much power over him? He was used to calling the tune, orchestrating his life and the women in it. Now a scrap of a female had him in tow. As much as she delighted him, his loss of control made him uneasy and irritated.

When he leaned down to kiss her, she nipped his lower lip with sharp teeth. "Don't get too used to doing that," she said. "I'm in your house, but that does not give you rights over me."

He straightened, rubbing his lips as he eyed her thoughtfully. What a paradox you are, Damiene, both arousing and hurtful. Could it be that you're not angry at my kissing you, but because I haven't kissed you enough?"

"You—you—" Amusement and embarrassment at his accurate comment warred in her. Still she couldn't contain a chuckle. "It's a wonder someone hasn't tried to execute you."

He stiffened, and his twisted smile couldn't hide the sudden tightening of his lips, the shuttering of his eyes.

"Piers?"

"Let me join you," he said. "I could use some of that fruit."

"No."

"No, I can't have fruit?"

"No, don't try to put me off. Did someone once try to kill you?"

"Yes." He popped a grape into his mouth.

The conversation was over, she thought. He wasn't going to say any more. Why had an attempt been made on his life? And why did it bother her so? Why did it make her scorchingly angry that someone would want to hurt this man?

"Anyone ever try to kill you?" he asked, his voice even. He saw the fluttering of surprise in her eyes, the infinitesimal drawing back. "Other than the car a few days ago, that is."

"What a question." His scrutiny was too sharp, and she looked away. "Do you ask everyone that?"

"No." She hadn't given him an answer, and he recognized the edge of panic in her voice.

Anxiously she tried to switch topics. "Do you have family in this area?"

"No. My last remaining relative died last year in England." And he hadn't mourned his uncle, who'd pulled more than one nasty trick to gain control of the legacy that had come to Piers from his deceased parents.

"Oh. I'm sorry."

"Don't be. Uncle Leland and I weren't close. And do you have family here?"

"No, my family lives back east. And I'm close to them."

At least she'd told him something about herself, he thought. "I'm having a party Saturday night. I'd planned it before we met."

"A party?"

"Yes. It's going to be at Vince's." He faced her, his gaze pinning her. "Will you be my hostess?"

"Ah, I don't think—"

"Don't say no. I want you to stay here. You told me you wanted to pay board—"

"And you keep telling me that you won't take money from me." Where would she go if she left Piers's, she wondered. She didn't want to leave Las Vegas yet. The search had brought her here. She might at last be able to find Barnaby Echo, the man who'd killed

Gilbert. And if she left the safety of Piers's home, Barnaby Echo—whoever he was—might find her first. Piers's voice pulled her from her thoughts.

"No, I won't take money from you," he was saying. "So, in lieu of board, why not act as my hostess? No strings. You'd be doing me a big favor."

"Why a party all of a sudden?"

Her question made a shutter snap down over his eyes. They were like rusted iron, jagged, opaque, dangerous. Although he spoke easily, wariness emanated from him.

"It's not that sudden. As I said I've been planning it. Will you be my hostess?"

He should be pushing her away, he told himself, suggesting she leave, not urging her to stay. The party was a way of possibly smoking out some information on Berto's death. A great many of the people who'd frequented his London club played in Las Vegas at this time of year. He hoped that by inviting some of them, idle conversation might reveal something. The smallest bit of information could help. A name, a place, anything that would give him a lead.

He looked at Damiene. His home was no sanctuary, nor would the party be a safer place. Too many people must know that he wouldn't rest until Berto's killer or killers were apprehended.

Reason told him it would be safer for Damiene away from him, out of Las Vegas. What magic did she have that negated his reason and good sense? And even if it was safer for her to be out of Las Vegas, where would she go? And would he ever be able to find her again?

"I've never been a hostess," she said, "except for the small parties I've given myself. What if I insult your guests, or pour water down their necks, or arm-wrestle them . . . ?"

"All of it sounds entertaining, and I'm sure you'd be a hit . . . but I think I'll hire a trio and you can be hostess instead." He pulled her close with one strong arm. "Say you'll do it."

"All right." It was a relief to know she'd have a place to stay for a while longer. That it was a delight as well, she didn't care to ponder. She wouldn't dwell on the attractions of Quicksilver Larraby. "What type of party will it be?" she asked.

"What kind do you like? Do you like magicians? How about a clown? Kissing booth?" Piers found it more enjoyable to look into her eyes than dwell on a party.

"That's silly." She took one firm step back. It was hard to breathe when that close to him.

"Then we'll settle on the original plan. A run-of-the-mill cocktail party."

Although he tried not to, he couldn't help recalling another cocktail party, this one in Sardinia. Diving off a terrace into the sea had not been one of his favorite things.

Damiene studied Piers closely. Why had his body turned to steel? What black memory stalked him? "Whatever you're thinking must be painful. Does it have something to do with the party?"

He forced a smile. "Another party. But I think I'll prefer the one we'll have." He touched a corner of her mouth with a finger. She was beautiful.

His silky tone had no warmth, she mused. And he had no intention of telling her about the other party. Piers Larraby seemed to have as many secrets as she. "I don't have a great many party clothes with me," she said, raising her hand to cup his jaw.

"Why don't you go downtown and charge—"

Abruptly she jerked her hand from his face.

"No!" she said firmly. "I'll wear what I have."

She walked toward the door. No way would she take any clothing or anything else from him. It was bad enough she was living in his house for free.

He moved quickly behind her, his arms slipping around her waist. "That was insensitive. Consider the offer withdrawn. Of course whatever you choose to wear will be fine."

"Thank you." She closed her eyes when his mouth roamed over her neck, his breath teasing tendrils of hair.

Quicksilver was known for its speed and its deadliness, she thought, especially when it entered the blood. Then it killed. She should be more careful. Quicksilver was a fantasy, and a brief one. But she would savor those moments with him while she could.

She turned in his arms, her own sliding up around his neck slowly, deliberately. When she felt his heart hammering against her, she was swept into the fantasy. It gripped her and spun her into a passion she hadn't even dreamed existed.

His mouth came down hard on hers as he dragged her against his body. He was still wearing only swim trunks, and his bare skin was hot to her touch. As she parted her lips to his demanding tongue, she wondered if he would scorch her. Brand her forever.

He groaned as their tongues tangled, and dropped his hands to cup her buttocks. He fit her more snugly against him, his lips nudging hers, and she gasped as fire swept through her at the intimate contact. No, she couldn't leave this man. Not yet . . .

"I've brought some drinks."

Damiene opened her eyes and looked over Piers's shoulder. Sure enough, Miguel was there with a jug and glasses. Thank God! Was she out of her mind? Within a hair of giving herself to this man!

His face bland, Miguel looked right at Damiene. "Plain or with ice?"

Piers continued to kiss her. Was he deaf? She pulled back with great effort, air rasping from her lungs. "Lots . . . of . . . ice." Gulping in deep breaths, she stared at the man above her.

"What? Ice? Why the hell—Miguel! Dammit!"

Damiene moved easily between the two men and took the drink Miguel was proferring. "Mmm, very nice. Cherry juice, isn't it? Delicious."

"I thought you might be thirsty after the munchies." Miguel spoke to Damiene but kept his gaze on Piers.

"Are you getting out of here, or do we go a few rounds?" Piers asked sweetly.

"Your choice," Miguel replied.

"I'm surprised you have such a good accent, Miguel," Damiene said, trying to break the tension as she eyed the two men uneasily. They were joking. Right?

"I've been in this country since the age of three," Miguel said. "I went to school here . . . among other things."

"I'll have some of that juice too," Piers said flatly. He gulped down the fruit juice, then slammed down the glass, turned, and dove into the pool.

"Touchy, isn't he?" Miguel said.

"Has he always been, Miguel?"

"Just lately." He grinned, showing a gap where a tooth had been

"You provoke him. Why?" She was staring over the rim of her glass at Piers as he swam up and down the pool as though a devil were riding him.

"It brings him back to life . . . just like you've done."

"Excuse me?" Damiene turned around to see Miguel disappearing through the doorway.

A party! Damiene thought two days later. More like a blooming celebrity convention. She could barely move through the throng of guests whose faces she'd seen on newscasts, movies, and television. Did Piers know everyone?

"That's Dolph Wakefield over there," she breathed, clutching Piers's arm. "He's considered the hottest heartthrob in the country right now."

"Is he? He doesn't do a thing for me," Piers said bitingly.

She looked up at him. "I thought you were friends."

"In most things we are." He kissed the tip of her nose. "Have I told you that I love that turquoise silk skirt on you?"

"Several times." She bloomed under his smile. "Tell me how you know a movie star like Dolph Wakefield."

"Actually, he thinks of himself as an actor, not a star." Piers's gaze focused on the imposingly tall blond man in the corner talking to a group of women. "And lately he's been doing some producing and directing. We met in Europe." He shook his head at the memory. "Dolph has a punishing right. One evening about ten years ago he used it to good advantage in a bistro in Paris. Three men with whom

I'd just shot dice decided to get their money back, and they jumped me. Dolph intervened. I had my nose broken, and Dolph busted a collar bone. I slept on his couch that night because my fellow players knew where I was staying."

"You're close to him."

"Yes. I trust him."

She looked at the actor again. "He's even better-looking in person. How old is he?"

"As old as the pyramids, I think."

She was going to ask what he meant, when a guest claimed his attention.

Wandering away, she looked around at the crowd. It was a good thing Piers had decided to have it here in Vince's, she thought. Even his home might have been stretched at the seams with such a large group.

The platinum and diamond set that was there was out of her league. She had known Piers was not an ordinary gambler, and not only from what he'd told her. She'd read bits of an article about him in an in-flight magazine on the plane from Atlantic City to Las Vegas. She'd learned that he owned a villa in Monaco, and that he jet-setted with European and American glitterati. But somehow it was still a surprise to see the collection of people at his party.

At first Damiene wasn't sure that the people she saw were the ones they resembled. When Miguel moved past her serving drinks, she detained him by taking one from the tray. "That man looks so familiar," she said, gesturing with her glass toward a husky man with dark chestnut hair. "I think I've seen him in *Today* magazine. Do you know him, Miguel?"

"Yes, that's Honey Bear Kenmore. Are you a racing fan?"

"No," she said slowly, her grin spreading. "But I saw those tabloid pictures of him on a beach in Nice."

"And when did you see those?" Piers asked. He had come behind her, taking a drink from the tray as well.

She looked up, amused. Her smile faded at the hard look on his face. "What is it? You look like you're in pain."

"No," he muttered.

"I think he is," Miguel said softly, before moving away.

Piers glared after him.

"Is Honey Bear Kenmore another friend of yours?" Damiene asked.

"Yes. Bear and I started out driving the circuit together after we graduated from Harvard. I had an accident and quit. Bear kept at it. He was the better driver anyway." Why, he wondered, did the thought of Damiene seeing one of his best friends naked make his stomach churn? "I guess I didn't know you were into pornography."

She bristled. "Tabloids are on most newsstands, Piers. Since when have you become so prissy and judgmental?" A globe-trotting professional gambler questioning her morals! How ironic.

"You're living in my house. I expect you to have some decorum."

"Decorum? What's that got to do with reading a tabloid while standing in line at the supermarket? I'll bet the back issues of most of them are full of *your* exploits."

"Don't assume." He shifted uncomfortably as he recalled a few incidents in his past, and that made his irritation bloom into temper. Why did he care so much about what she did and thought? When had he ever cared about any woman that much?

"You—you jackass," she sputtered. Before he could move, she brought her heel down hard on his foot and stalked away.

Dolph Wakefield strolled across the room, his glance flicking from Damiene to Piers's rigid back. "Nice step," he drawled, eyeing Piers as he clutched his foot. "Get it from a one-legged hen? I would have thought you'd have saved it for the dancing."

Honey Bear Kenmore came up on Piers's other side, studying his friend. "Very sexy lady. And her footwork's not bad either."

"Shut up, Bear." Piers glared at Dolph, who was trying to smother his amusement, then turned his scowl on Bear. "Do you enjoy making an exhibition of yourself in the tabloids?"

Dolph's brows rose, his gaze sliding toward the terrace where Damiene had just disappeared, then he looked back at his disgruntled friend. "Well, well. Did the lady see Bear in his ah, *altogether*, as they say?"

Bear put a well-muscled arm in front of Piers when he rounded on Dolph. "Since that was some time ago, and you know I didn't realize those pictures had been taken until the feature appeared, something got to you. You've never commented on it before, so I have to come to the same conclusion as Dolph. Did the luscious creature who attempted to slice through your foot with her stiletto heel make some remark? Did she like my pecs?" His voice was filled with humor.

"Maybe." Piers's eyes narrowed dangerously.

"She must have, Bear," Dolph said. "Perhaps she mentioned your buns as well."

"No doubt."

"Not funny." Piers's teeth were clenched together.

"No, but you are, my man," Dolph said. "What's up? Anyone would think you're in love with yon fair maiden."

"I agree," Bear added. "Haven't seen you this heated up in a while. If ever."

Piers's hands flexed into fists. No! He couldn't let that happen. Not love.

Bear straightened from his indolent stance. "You're white as a sheet, Piers. What is it?"

"Must be something I ate." Love! he thought. When had it happened? The night they sailed over the cacti! Damn. "I'll talk to Vince."

"Did you think you'd be immune to the slings and arrows of outrageous love, to paraphrase the poet?" Dolph asked softly.

Piers stiffened. "You take some shots, chum."

"I've been known to be a tad satirical."

Dolph's worldly, lazy smile didn't fool Piers. He was well aware of his friend's loyalty.

"Is that it?" Bear asked, grinning. "How does it feel, Quicksilver? I didn't think mercury got that high." His smile widened when Piers turned to face him, the glint in his eyes feral. "Uh-oh."

"Easy, you two," Dolph said. "I admit that a free-for-all would relieve the boredom, but aren't we looking for, hoping for, something to happen this evening?"

Bear nodded, his amiable look hardening into chiseled power. "Anybody special arrive?" He looked around him, his smile genial, his eyes probing. "Well, well, there's Rustam. You said he'd come, Piers. I didn't believe he would."

Piers glanced around, gazing at the man who had seemed to be on the periphery of his life for many years. Had he arranged Berto's death? The gambler turned "financial adviser" had the clout, and he'd hated Piers and his partner for a long time because he'd lost his gambling clientele to them almost from the moment their London club had opened.

"You and Berto made an enemy when you all but wiped out his gambling revenues," Dolph said.

"He was cheating his clientele. He deserved to go bust."

"But you shouldn't have thrown him out of your club when he came to play," Bear said, his grin twisted.

"He tried cheating in our place. I should've broken every bone in his body."

"You did break his nose," Bear said.

"And he was in London at the time of the fire," Dolph said tightly.

"Yeah." Piers flexed his hands into fists. "If I thought—"

"Easy, man," Bear said quietly. "Maybe we'd better mix with the guests. No sense causing speculation."

"I think I'd like to talk to Mr. Rustam Dever," Dolph murmured as he moved away.

Bear nodded to Piers and followed.

Piers looked toward the club terrace. He had to talk to Damiene. And examine his own feelings. Love! It was a shock. Greeting guests but not stopping to talk, she headed for the double doors leading to the club terrace.

Damiene stood outside on the terrace. The night was warm, but she felt chilled. It was time for her to leave. Obviously that was what Piers wanted. Why else would he lash out at her? Hurt was a sword thrust through her middle. She knew she would never forget Las Vegas . . . or Piers Larraby.

"Hello."

Damiene swiped at the tears on her face and turned, smiling mechanically. "Hello, my name is . . . But I know you."

The crooked smile on the man's face widened, and he nodded. "Yes. I'm flattered you remembered. Our first meeting was very fleeting."

"You're Vince Dalrymple from England."

"Yes, but I've been in this country for a couple of years." He paused. "I trust all of your belongings were intact the other night."

"Yes, thank you, Mr. Dalrymple."

"Please call me Vince. Most people do." He moved closer to her and leaned against the railing of the terrace. "Piers is a good man, a bit of a loner, but a good, loyal friend."

Was Vince Dalrymple giving her a message of sorts, she wondered. "Loner? I don't see him that way. Everything he does is with other people, sometimes crowds of them." She laughed shortly. "This party is a circus."

"True, but not much really touches him. Few people know him. He's been my friend for years, and I'm not sure I know every facet of him. No, I'll amend that. I'm sure there are layers of him that I'll never know." He settled himself on one of the built-in benches. "Have you enjoyed living in Las Vegas?"

She studied him in the kaleidoscopic light coming from the club. "It's been . . . interesting," she said cautiously.

"Piers is interesting. He and my brother were at Oxford together. Piers was a Rhodes scholar."

"What?" Although he was intelligent, Piers had never struck her as a scholar.

"Yes, he's very bright. Albert, my brother, had always said Piers was head and shoulders over many of the other students, and could have been a don at Oxford had he chosen such a route."

"Why would a Rhodes scholar become a gambler? Somehow it doesn't fit."

Vince laughed softly. "No, I suppose it doesn't. I do know that Piers was considered something of a genius at business, fascinated with percentages and such."

"Other men have the same gifts. It doesn't lead them to be professional gamblers."

"No, but then, Piers is not at all like other men."

Neither heard the terrace door slide open, so both jumped at the sound of Piers's voice. "You two seem to be having fun. Is this a private party?"

Damiene heard the irritation in his tone and reacted to it. Hands curling into fists, she turned to face him.

Vince stood up slowly. "You seem a bit put out, Piers."

"Maybe."

"In that case, perhaps I should collect Miss Belson and take her to my place."

"That won't be necessary," Piers said flatly.

"Ooo, temper. Miguel said you were a little off color."

"Very funny."

"I guess I'll talk to Bear and Dolph. They're no doubt in better spirits. I assume they're inside."

"Yes."

The sound of the sliding door opening and closing was like a slap in the stillness. Piers looked after the retreating Vince even when he had melted into a group of people inside the club room. Then he turned to Damiene, who was staring at him.

"I was looking for you," he said softly. She stiffened, and he stretched his hand toward her, then let it drop to his side. "I apologize."

She blinked in surprise.

"Aren't you going to say anything?" he asked.

"I—I had just about made up my mind to leave. I thought that might be easier for both of us."

"No! Don't let my careless words drive you away. I said I was sorry."

"So am I." She finally looked into his eyes.

"Stay with me," he whispered, moving close and taking her in his arms. Kissing her had become a sustaining force in his life, a salve, a necessity. Even if she were furious with him, he knew he'd need to hold her and caress her.

She clung to him, her fingers digging into his back. Heat assaulted her senses.

The kiss deepened.

His hands slid down to her buttocks. He lifted her up and closer, his fingers massaging her, her silk skirt feeling erotic beneath his hands.

Fitted to his aroused body, Damiene felt an overwhelming flood of passion. At the same time, she felt as if this were a homecoming, the excitement he sparked in her as familiar as her own name. What an paradox of emotions Piers Larraby called forth from her. In short order—days, for heaven sake— he'd become the focus in her life.

"Damiene." Piers pulled his mouth from hers, resting his damp forehead against her hair, his breath rasping in her ear.

"Piers." Never had she felt such cataclysmic sensations.

"Are you all right?"

She nodded, not moving from his arms, but settling slowly back onto the planet. "Hadn't you better see to your guests? They'll think you've done a bunk."

"What an old-fashioned phrase." He caressed her face, touching her brows, running a finger down the straight nose, circling her tender lips. "I want to stay with you until you tell me you won't leave me. What do *you* want?"

Blood thudded through her. "I . . . I . . ." Her breath was short. "I want to stay with you."

"Good. Let's go in and mingle with our guests . . . together."

After once more kissing her thoroughly, Piers led her back into the club.

They were circulating through the room, chatting with various guests, when two handsome men moved in front of Damiene.

"You're Damiene," the blond one said.

"And you're Dolph Wakefield, the movie star." She saw his obvious wince and smiled. "Would it have been better to say actor extraordinaire?"

"By far preferable." Dolph's gaze slid to his friend. "Piers, my man, you may have found a gem."

"I have."

"Then she'd probably prefer me," the other man said. "Damiene, I'm Bear."

"How do you do." She shook his hand.

Piers fixed his friend with a long, hard look. "Don't push your luck, Bear."

"Oh?" He looked at Dolph. "He obviously has no humor where the lovely lady is concerned."

"Piers, stop it," Damiene said. Half amused, half appalled, she gazed up at him. "You're crazy."

"I'll do better," he muttered.

"I don't think so," Dolph said, smiling when Piers scowled at him. "This is a lovely party, Damiene. Piers said you helped him plan it."

"A small part of it. Thank you. It was fun." And it had been, she mused. It had been weeks since she'd been able to do anything so frivolous, so distracting from her mission.

"And I think we should enjoy some of the fruits of our labors and dance," Piers announced.

"You sound like you're going to a hanging," she murmured, wondering why he was so tense.

"Dancing is very good way to work off frustration, Damiene. I think we both need it."

She raised her brows. "Pompous ass."

"Sounds like she might prefer dancing with me," Bear said. "I'm very good, Damiene."

"Not with a broken leg," Piers said silkily.

"Don't bait him, Bear," Dolph said. "Vince wouldn't like it if we broke up his club room. We'll join the others at cards." He indicated a group gathered around a table in the far corner of the room. "It was pleasure to meet you, Damiene."

She smiled. "It was nice meeting both of you."

Piers saw another one of his prime suspects at the card table. He nodded slowly. "Playing cards is a good idea."

Dolph followed his glance and smiled.

Damiene looked toward the card table, puzzled.

Bear leaned over and kissed her on the cheek. "It was nice to meet you, Damiene. See you soon, my quicksilver friend. Stay low."

Piers nodded tautly.

"What did Bear mean?" Damiene asked. "About you staying low, that is." She watched as Piers's face tightened, his eyes turning opaque.

"Inside joke."

"Are you hiding something from me, Quicksilver Larraby?" She felt threatened because he was. It hurt to think of him in danger.

"Shall we exchange confidences?" he asked, watching as she glanced around the room as though checking for friend or enemy.

"I guess we have to accept that it would be better not to bare our souls to each other," she replied. His look seemed to peel away the protective layers she'd surrounded herself with. "Since we do have secrets from each other, perhaps it would be better if I found someplace else—"

"This is the best place for you to be. We settled that," he said abruptly, leading her onto the section of floor set aside for dancing. Pulling her close, he let both his arms settle around her tightly.

"We didn't settle anything," she said, trying to put a little space between them.

"Yes, we did. You'd stay here and give me a hand—"

"The party's doing well—"

"—and help manage things around my house, and that would take care of your board."

"I should continue going to the casinos every day." Her gaze slid away from his.

His eyes narrowed. "We've done that." And he'd been very curious about her reasons for it. They had gone to three different casinos in the past three nights. He had stayed close to her, not questioning when she abruptly left one table for another, even when she was winning. And she never seemed to care very much about how much she won. The few times he left her to get another drink or to speak to someone he knew, he would watch her talk to the dealer, apparently asking him a question. Invariably the dealer would shake his head and she'd sink back in her chair, disappointed. Piers was certain she wasn't in Las Vegas to gamble. She was seeking something . . . or someone.

"Why do you gamble?" he asked softly.

She didn't answer.

"Another secret? Damiene?"

"Yes, it's something I don't wish to discuss with you." She couldn't tell him about Gilbert. It might endanger him.

"All right, we have some hidden things between us. Accept that. I have." His arms tightened convulsively. Could she be searching for a man? A man she loved?

"Easy," she said, wriggling in his hard embrace. "I do need to breathe." Actually she liked his tight hold, welcomed it. But if she stayed too close, the gambler with ice in his veins could melt her. Piers Larraby was dry ice, burning her defenses with cold.

"Let me into your life, darling," he murmured, bending his head down and flicking his tongue over her lips.

"You're already there," she said weakly. Holding him to her, she kissed him, wanting him, loving him, knowing she couldn't keep him.

When she broke free and strode quickly off the dance floor, Piers stared after her, wild-eyed. "Damiene." Her name was a tortured whisper.

Damiene had no destination in mind. She had to be alone. When she pushed open a door leading to the parking lot, she breathed a sigh of relief.

For a moment she thought she was alone, then she saw a lighted cigarette in the shadow of the building. She stepped back.

"Don't worry, ma'am." The figure moved forward into the light. "My name's Greg Tillson. I'm a dealer at Vince's"

She impulsively walked over to him. "Have you ever been a dealer in Atlantic City? At the Nugget?"

He smiled, shaking his head. "No, ma'am. I haven't been in Atlantic City in many years."

Disappointment shook her, though she told herself she should be used to the answer. It seemed that no one in Las Vegas had been to Atlantic City in a long time. And no one had ever heard of Barnaby Echo.

Greg Tillson stamped out his cigarette. "Sorry, I can see it's important to you—"

They both turned when the door to the casino banged open.

Piers stood there, his fists clenched. He approached Tillson slowly.

Damiene stared at him open-mouthed for a moment, then she rushed to him. "Stop it. You're acting like a lion with a sore paw. Let's get back inside."

"How do you know him?"

She grabbed an arm, its muscles taut. "If you don't go back in there with me at once, I'll—I'll leave Las Vegas."

He stared down at her, then turned stiffly and retraced his steps.

Damiene kept her hold on his arm.

Though they stayed together until the last guest departed and it was time to leave, neither said much to the other.

Anger simmered between them.

Three

_____

"Dammit," Piers exploded the next morning, "you know that was a dangerous thing to do last night. What made you go out to the parking lot with that guy? Do you realize you could have been in deep trouble?" He glared at Damiene.

"He was already there when I went outside," she snapped back. "I was asking him something." And it had been a waste of time. "You frightened him to death when you came on like gangbusters."

"I didn't know if you were all right," Piers said stiffly.

"I thought he might know something. I would have been back in the casino in two minutes if you hadn't come roaring out of the place."

"I didn't do that."

"You did."

They stared at each other for a long moment.

"You were like King Kong on a rampage." A giggle escaped Damiene, then a laugh. "Don't . . . think

. . . I'm not . . . angry with you." Tears trickled from her eyes as her laughter increased. "You're pouting."

"Dammit, Damiene, I don't pout." Reluctant laughter rippled from his throat and he pulled her into his arms. "I was worried when you just walked away from me and disappeared."

"I wanted to be alone, but I should have told you where I was."

His mouth met hers with fierce gentleness, in a long, searching kiss. "Yes."

Breathless, she stared up at him, her hand cupping his jaw. "I will next time."

"Tonight? I think I'll go to someplace other than Vince's tonight. Want to come along?"

"Yes." She smiled and murmured, "My luck's been good lately.

The next few days were quiet. Although Piers still holed up in his study every morning, he devoted his afternoons and evenings to Damiene. They would lunch together, then sometimes take a long drive, one day traveling down to Death Valley. Another day she talked him into going to a casino early. She knew dealers worked different shifts, and if she went only at night she would never get the chance to talk to many of them. In the evenings they would often dine at home, then go to the casinos, sometimes hitting two or three in one night. Damiene could sense Piers's curiosity about her insisting she gamble whenever she could, and was eternally thankful he never asked her questions she couldn't answer.

No matter what they did, the fiery sensual awareness between them simmered beneath the surface.

Just the lightest touch of Piers's hand on hers made Damiene wonder if she would burst into flames. Ever since the night of the party, when they had danced and she had realized she was so close to loving him, she had longed to tear down all the barriers between them and give herself to him, heart, body, and soul, for as long, for as long as he wanted her. Yet there was a strange reserve in him now, as if he, too, had stepped close to the passionate fire, and had decided to keep back, for fear of being burned.

Late one morning, as she was reading in the sunny living room, she glanced up to catch him staring speculatively at her. As always, desire rose instantly within her at the sight of him. She looked away, fearing he'd see the arousal in her eyes.

"What shall we do today?" she asked.

Piers shook his head slightly, her question startling him out of his musings about her. Why was she still such a mystery, he wondered. Despite the closeness he felt between them, she held back from him. Not for the first time he wished his own life was unencumbered so that he could plumb the secrets of the most intriguing woman he'd met in years— Damiene Belson. He wanted to know everything about her. He could never know enough.

He strode into the room. "I thought tonight we could get all gussied up and have a special dinner here, just the two of us."

"I'd like that." Damiene was always a little horrified at the amount of money Piers spent when they went out. He certainly seemed able to afford it, which was more than she could say for herself. Her savings were nearly depleted, and she'd been trying to live on her winnings when she met Piers. Her partner was still running their small accounting firm, with her father's help, but there was no money to spare there. A sense of weariness suddenly welled up within her as she thought of how long he had been searching for Gilbert's killer, how long she'd been away from her home and family.

What was wrong, Piers wondered, seeing the sadness fill her eyes. What was she thinking? "Would you like to swim now?" he asked, hoping to distract her.

"Yes," she said as she stood up. "I'm feeling in need of some exercise."

"You're quite a contender in the pool," he said, taking her hand as they strolled from the room. "Swim for your college?"

"Yep, went to the nationals once, and Gil—" She stopped abruptly and looked away from him.

"Don't want to tell me too much?" he asked, a familiar pang of regret piercing him.

She nodded. "What a strange pair we are, hiding from each other the way we do."

"But good friends too."

Startled, she gazed up at him. "How can that be when we argue so much, hide so much?"

"Most intelligent people disagree some of the time. Only zombies always concur. We're more than comfortable with each other, aren't we?"

"Yes," she said slowly. "I guess we are."

"You know we are, so admit it." Sweeping her up into his arms, he ran down the hall to the solarium.

"Where are you going? What are you doing?" She struggled to free herself, then grew still as he stopped by the pool. "No! Don't you dare!"

"You never should have said *dare*, darling." Without hesitation he jumped into the water with Damiene in his arms.

"Fool!" she sputtered when her head broke water. She swiped the hair from her eyes. "My skirt is wool."

"I'll buy you another."

"You bet your life you will. You owe me." She cupped her hand and slapped a sheet of water into his face, then swam to the side and levered herself out of the pool. She looked back at him. "I should bash you."

He grinned, leaning his arms on the side, making no effort to get out. "Your breasts heave beautifully when you're angry."

"Pervert." She looked down at herself and realized her blouse was now see-through, her nipples quite clear against the wet material. "Ohhh." Pivoting on her heel, she squished across the tile floor.

"We'll shop for a new outfit this afternoon."

"You're right about that," she shot over her shoulder.

"You look beautiful wet."

His low voice carried to her like a clarion call, stiffening her spine, hurrying her. His chuckle trailed behind her.

In her room she stripped off the soggy clothes, grimacing at her once-good pair of low-heeled leather shoes. He could replace those too. But even as she was cursing him, she couldn't stem the chuckle that rose up in her. Piers Larraby made her laugh.

She had just donned a robe when there was a knock at the door. "Who is it?"

"It's me," Miguel said.

"Wait a minute." She crossed to the door and opened it.

"I thought I could take care of your shoes and clothes for you." His mouth twisted upward. "I understand you swam in them."

"Pretty funny, huh?"

"Yeah, it is."

She scooped up her wet things and handed them to him. "I think they're ready for the dumpster."

"Maybe. We'll see. Piers says to get dressed and you'll lunch downtown and shop."

"Well, you can tell him—"

"Tell him yourself," Miguel said, and walked away.

"Bozo."

Torn between getting a replacement for the ensemble she'd used for travel and daywear, and putting Piers in his place by telling him a few things, she argued with herself all during her shower and dressing.

She had to do her makeup twice because she made a sudden gesture when talking to herself and smudged mascara across her cheek.

Finally ready, she opened her door and saw Piers propped against the opposite wall. "What are you doing here?" she asked.

"What kept you?"

"You kept me," she snapped. "You make me talk to myself."

"Interesting. Any other members of your family afflicted?" Teasing her was more arousing than being in bed with another woman? Crazy.

"Amusing."

He smiled, his gaze flicking over her. She looked wonderful in the apricot cotton dress and low-heeled slip-ons. He touched her arm. "Very nice. The color suits you."

"Thank you." His light caress made her long to hurl herself into his arms. Instead, she stepped back. "Where will we go?"

"There's a little shop downtown that's quite good," he said as he led her out of the house.

"And you would know about women's fashions," she muttered, slipping into the car.

He smothered a smile at her jealous tone as he slid behind the wheel. "Damiene, how you talk. This woman happens to be a friend of mine."

She glanced at him suspiciously, but said no more as they drove into Las Vegas. When he turned onto a relatively quiet, narrow side street, she looked around curiously.

"Where are—no! Not here. I couldn't afford a swatch from here."

Piers parked the car in front of the discreet establishment with champagne-colored drapes on the window and the couturière's name scrolled in gold on the door. "Don't be silly," he said. "Charine is a friend of mine. She'll be glad to help you choose something." He grinned at her. "Besides, I'm buying, since I ruined your skirt."

"True. But I still don't wear clothes from designer salons." Damiene looked at the storefront again. "I knew she had places on the East and West coasts, but I'd never heard of one of her shops being here."

She glared at Piers as he helped her from the car. "Run up quite a bill here, do you? Well, I don't want to be lumped with your stable of women."

All of her life she had been a calm, stable, easygoing person. Now, ever since meeting Piers, her emotions were in constant turmoil, her temper seeming to flare regularly every hour. Like now. Thinking about the other women he must have known was way down on her list of things she wanted to do.

"Relax," he said. "You'll get an acid stomach."

"I've had one since meeting you."

"That's not true. You eat everything and anything like a lumberjack and are never bothered."

"Ohhh, how like you to make a remark about my healthy appetite." She lifted her chin and sailed past him when he opened the door, the light tinkling of a bell signaling their presence.

"Was I being ungentlemanly?" he murmured, following her.

His teasing voice set her skin to tingling. He'd tricked her into Charine's by baiting her! She'd been so busy fuming at him, she'd walked right into the salon. "You—"

A woman came through a curtained area to one side of the room. "May I help you?" she asked, a small smile on her face.

"May we speak with Charine?" Piers asked.

"I'm sorry, sir, Madame is in New York."

Damiene turned to the door. "That's it. Time to go."

Piers grabbed her arm. "Wait." He looked back at the woman, smartly coiffed and dressed all in black. "Perhaps you could help us. My name is Piers Larraby."

The woman's tight, polite expression softened, the smile widening fractionally. "Of course, sir. If you would come this way into the back. I can get you coffee or tea. Or perhaps you'd prefer white wine." The woman turned to Damiene. "You take a size eight, I think."

Damiene nodded without thinking.

"We'd like tea, please," Piers said, and gestured for Damiene to follow the woman.

"Sultan," she muttered.

"I heard that."

"Too bad."

They entered a small circular showroom. The woman instructed them to sit on the plush chairs, then disappeared through a curtain beside the runway. A young girl bought in a tray of tea things, served them, then she, too, disappeared. Within moments the room dimmed so that the short runway and the curtain in front of it were highlighted.

"We're going to have a show? For a skirt?" Appalled, Damiene looked toward the exit.

"Of course," Piers said. "How else would you choose an outfit?"

"I generally go up to a rack or counter, pick a few things, try them on, then make a choice."

"Clever. Shh, here's the first one. Ah, now, that's nice. What do you think?"

"This is crazy. That's a silk dress suitable for an intimate party of two hundred at the Ritz-Carlton."

"No need to get edgy, just look at them." Was it the end of the world if he gave something to her, he wondered. After all, he owed the skirt to her.

"I am looking and there's nothing that—oh, look at that." Peach-colored silk trousers with a camisole top in the same fabric delineated the slender figure of the model. "My, wouldn't that be grand." Damiene sighed. "But I want something more tailored, something I can use for all occasions."

"That looks useful to me." Piers made an almost infinitesimal gesture, and the dark-haired woman in black, watching from beside the runway, nodded.

"Lord, Piers, these fabrics are lovely. Oooo, look at that skirt and silk blouse in champagne."

Again Piers made the gesture.

When the show ended fifteen minutes later, Damiene jumped to her feet. "See? I told you there wouldn't be anything here."

"So you did." Piers stood and touched her nose with one finger. "It would be delightful to buy you a wardrobe." The slight smile on her face tightened, and she started to draw back from him. He took hold of her upper arms. "Hasn't it occurred to you that I might have honorable intentions?"

He was sure the surprise on her face was mirrored on his own. Although he still oversaw the running of his various businesses, nothing had been allowed to interfere with his search for Berto's killers. Yet, having Damiene at his side the last several days had opened wide his life, given it new dimension, a sparkle he hadn't even known was missing.

Honorable intentions? Damiene thought, staring at him. Toward her? She couldn't stem the hot tide that suffused her, even as she pulled back from him. How could she want him so much when she knew she couldn't have him?

As they reentered the main room of the salon, Damiene was startled when the dark-haired woman handed Piers a box. "What's that?"

"A box. Shall we go?" Piers ushered her out to the street.

"Will you stop that? You're pushing me."

"No, I'm not, I'm just hurrying you along. Thought you might be hungry."

"If you make one more reference to my appetite . . ."

"I wasn't doing that. Are you hungry?"

"Yes, but—"

"There you are." He opened the passenger door of the car and flung the box in the back before helping her into the seat.

"What's in the box?" she asked as he got in behind the wheel.

"Clothes. I think you'll like this restaurant. It's French and they do a bouillabaisse that makes you think of a harbor café in Marseille."

"I've never been to Marseille."

He glanced at her. "No? I'll take you there someday." If there was ever a time in his life when he wasn't looking over his shoulder and every which way, he'd take her.

"Sounds wonderful," she said. It was downright magical to imagine traveling through France with Piers. If only they could forget their secrets and go now!

Lunch was delightful. Damiene kept looking around her, drinking in the delightful Gallic decor. Piers watched her, enjoying her enjoyment, her pleasure filling him with the same.

"You're eating as much as ever," he said as she finished the excellent bouillabaisse, "so I guess I can assume you like it."

"I enjoy fish stew," she said, baiting him. She put her spoon down and prepared to tell him he had to take back the clothes he'd bought at Charine's. She was a woman who bought for herself what she wanted and needed. She had just opened her mouth when she saw him glance behind her. His features tightened, and she looked over her shoulder.

"Friend of yours?" she asked. The man was a study in shiny black, from his fedora to the pointed toes of his shoes, as though someone had given him a shoeshine from eyebrow to ankle.

"Someone I know," Piers said shortly.

"Would you like to ask him to join us?" She glanced at the man again, vaguely remembering him from the party.

"No, I wouldn't."

"Who is he?"

"Rustam Dever."

She frowned. "I've heard that name."

Piers stiffened. Had she heard him talking to Bear and Dolph at the party? "Many people have. He used to own several small casinos in this town, along with a couple in the Caribbean and one in London. Nowadays he does most of his gambling on Wall Street."

"Now I remember. I read an article about a big deal he helped put together."

"Yes."

"Have you done business with him?"

"I've gambled in his houses."

"But you don't like him."

Piers shrugged. "Let's say I admire the flexibility of the man, the way he rides the razor's edge and never gets cut, his business acumen. He's made several fortunes." He smiled tightly, glancing at Dever once more before his gaze settled on Damiene. "Are you finished?"

"Yes."

"Shall we go?"

There was a constraint between them on the ride back to the house. It was as though, Damiene mused, Piers had eaten a poor meal rather than an exceedingly fine one. Had Rustam Dever put him in such a mood?

"Piers?"

"Yes."

"I think it's time for me to move on and—"

"We covered that." He reached over and put his hand on her knee. "You've been happy at the house, haven't you?"

Happy? Beyond happy, she'd found an overriding joy with Piers. "Yes."

Relief flooded him. "There you are. So we both accept the status quo. All right?"

"All right."

"And no more talk of leaving. Please."

"All right."

He threaded his fingers through hers, and kept them like that until he had to shift at a stoplight. He wanted her in his life, more each day. She was all the sunshine he had, and he needed her warmth and light.

He parked the car in front of the house and reached behind him for the box. Then he was out of the car and striding swiftly to the front door. "Last one in the pool," he called over his shoulder, "sets the table and makes dinner tonight. It's Miguel's night off." He raced into the house.

"Wait a minute! Cheater!" Swinging her purse over her shoulder, Damiene sped after him, amused and angry at the same time.

In the foyer she skidded to a stop on the tile floor. There were swimsuits in the changing room in the solarium. Miguel had shown them to her. "We'll see who sets the table and fixes dinner tonight, Mr. Larraby," she said strongly.

She ran down the hall to the solarium. Opening the cupboard in the changing room, she grabbed the first suit her hand touched. Quickly she stripped off her clothes, then pulled on the one-piece as fast as she could. "It doesn't cover much," she muttered. "Damn near cut up to the armpit on the side." And it dipped almost to the navel in front. Sighing, she snatched up her goggles and cap and ran from the cubicle.

She heard the sound of someone coming fast down the hallway. Tossing aside goggles and cap, she surged across the tile, then threw herself forward in a racing dive. She hit the water just in front of Piers.

Breaking the surface, she flung her hair back, laughing. "Guess who gets to cook tonight, and set the table."

"Damn! You remembered about the suits in here, didn't you?" Piers swam closer, loving the happy glitter to her eyes, the carefree expression on her face. Damiene Belson loved competition, and she was a damned good competitor. "The cat that ate the cream, that's you."

"Sore loser." She chuckled and clipped a sheet a water at him with the edge of her hand.

"Want to play, do you?" Dropping beneath the surface, he thrust himself at her.

Trying to maneuver away too late, Damiene took a deep breath, figuring she would be getting a good ducking. When she was pulled under and Piers's lips met hers, she gasped and almost lost her air. He breathed into her mouth, and her body became as liquid as the pool. She would have sunk to the bottom had not his hands tightened on her waist.

They surfaced together, mouths fused, legs and arms entwined.

Damiene leaned back. "Miguel . . . might . . . come."

Stars and planets wheeled behind her eyes, and the world had tipped.

"No. It's his night on the town. He won't come home until tomorrow morning."

"Oh."

They sank beneath the surface again.

This time Damiene curled her arms around his neck, holding him as tightly as he held her.

They surfaced again, Piers's long, strong legs keeping them afloat.

"I'm not letting you go this time," he told her huskily.

"I don't want you to," she whispered.

"God, I've wanted you since we cartwheeled over those cacti." He swam over to the side, still holding her.

"I've wanted you, too, but you should know there can be no commitments." It hurt to say that to him.

He hadn't expected such wrenching pain at her words. "I was going to say that to you." His smile was twisted. "We're outside the mainstream, aren't we, Damiene love?"

"Yes." She stifled a gasp of hurt.

Her wide-eyed acceptance hit him like a spear. He'd hurt her as she'd hurt him. How could the world be allowed to separate them? "We're agreed on no commitment?"

"Yes." She felt as if she were bleeding inside. But she'd always known there could be no future for them.

"Will you be my lover, Damiene Belson?"

His words feathered over her like a caress as he stroked her shoulder. She could refuse him nothing.

"Yes . . . but I don't know for how long."

"A day, a year, a millennium, we'll work on it."

She lifted one finger and pressed it against his lips, loving the tender toughness of that mouth. Her heart hammered against her ribs when he took her finger into his mouth and sucked gently. "It's a long shot," she said. "The two of us, I mean."

"Life's a long shot, lady." He pulled her close, suddenly wanting to put everything behind him except Damiene. His life had been one-dimensional before she entered it. Now he wanted the joy she brought him forever.

She nestled in his arms and gently bit his earlobe. A shiver coursed through him, and she chuckled.

"Like that?" she asked throatily. She loved doing it. Had there ever seen such a man as Piers Larraby? He bound her to him. She wanted him as she'd never wanted anyone. Her forays into sex had been minimal and lusterless, and it had been no trouble to ignore men. With Piers she was caught, and she hoped he never set her free.

"Yes, I like that," he murmured. "May I do it to you?"

"Yes." She could barely breathe. She knew she should run, yet she'd never thrown herself at anything more eagerly. If she died tomorrow, at least she'd have had the man she loved.

Love! No. That was ridiculous. Love didn't catapult into your life. It took years of cherishing, care, devotion. Love didn't blossom in just days . . . did it?

"Why so pensive?" Piers asked.

"Oh, I suppose I'm trying to find a viable reason for us to be together."

He kissed her gently. "And have you?"

"No. Have you?"

"I don't need to. Wanting you more than any woman I've ever known is enough for me."

"We have secrets from each other."

"Yes."

"Can a relationship be built on deceit?"

"No. But this isn't deceit. We're being up front about the secrets we have."

"And that's a little bit like splitting hairs, I think."

He stared at her for a long moment, then said, "We'd better get out of this pool before we look like prunes." Taking hold of her waist, he lifted her to the pool surround, then followed her up. His gaze was hot and intense on her face, then he turned away. "I'm going to take a shower. Why don't you do the same?" He started walking to the men's changing room. "I'll only be minute."

She bit her lip, watching him leave. He said he wanted her, and that was reason enough for him for them to be together. But it wasn't reason enough for her.

Four

Standing in the spacious women's section of the shower room, Damiene soaped her body pensively, wondering how easily Piers could accept their limited relationship.

"Room for one more?"

She stiffened at the sound of his voice behind her. "I thought this was the women's shower."

"It is, but since there's only the two of us in the house, I figured it would be all right. Besides, I wanted to talk to you."

"In the shower?"

"Admittedly it will be a distraction."

The slow, sensuous note in his voice made her turn to him. She faced him proudly, without embarrassment. "Will it?"

"You are being overtly tempting, Damiene Belson," he murmured, his gaze roving over her hungrily. It lingered on her full breasts, their coral tips tightening under his scrutiny. "You're too beautiful, my sweet." His gaze skimmed down her long legs, then he closed his eyes for a moment and took a deep breath. "Too potent."

Damiene was doing some avid staring herself. Looking at him gave her immeasurable delight. His body was hard and solid, dark hair curling across his broad chest and feathering down his strong legs. If he were a marble statue, he would be more revered than Michelangelo's "David."

He walked slowly to her, and her breath caught at his grace and power. He took the loofah sponge from her and began rubbing it sensually, erotically, over her body.

"What else do you do for a living beside gamble, Damiene Belson?" he asked in a husky voice.

The question threw her off stride even more than the delicious feel of his hand smoothing over her wet skin.

"Work? Oh . . . yes, I—I've been partners with one other person in an accounting firm that we started, doing taxes and financial planning mostly. We're working hard to establish ourselves, so there's not a great deal of recreation time in my life. Why do you ask?"

"I haven't had that much free time in my life either, though I know it looks as though my life is pure hedonism and nothing more."

"I don't know where this conversation is heading," she said, and she really didn't care. His hands were doing wild things to her body, cupping her breasts, stroking the soft flesh of her thighs. Heat was building in her like a blast furnace about to explode.

"The point I'm making," he said, nipping her neck, "is that neither of us has had that much leisure time. So I'm suggesting we put the real world on hold."

"I can't do that." Her body swayed, and she struggled to stay upright and not collapse in his arms. "I have an obligation to—"

"I'm not suggesting either of us disregard our responsibilities." He turned her so her back was to him and dragged the sponge down her body, between her breasts, across her stomach, lower . . . "Just," he added, his tone maddeningly calm, "that we put them on hold for a little while."

She bit back a moan. "I don't know if it's possible to let go of the world that way."

"It won't be easy. What do you say we try?" He ran his tongue across her shoulder, and his voice deepened seductively. "On even ground, meeting for the first time, with no barriers, caring about each other, going with that feeling."

"It's nonsense, absurd—"

His arms encircled her waist, and he lightly caressed her thigh with the sponge.

"But will you do it?"

She inhaled shakily. "What a concept, just doing nothing but savoring the moment."

"Yes. I want to try."

"Hedonist."

"Maybe."

"How long?"

"As long as we can."

"Oh."

The loofah fell to the floor and his hand grasped her thigh. "You're like velvet, Damiene."

Closing her eyes, she let the passion finally take her. "Am I?"

He turned in his arms. "You haven't answered my question."

"I'd like to try." She moaned as he nestled her lips against his. "But—"

"No buts, darling."

All other words were caught in her throat as his mouth came down on hers, its gentle ferocity worrying her lips apart. He sent the planet spinning and flung the moon and stars into an alien, sensual orbit . . . and he took her there with him.

Their tongues dueling, he held her tightly, their bodies swaying in the flood of passion. God, he wanted her, needed her. "Darling," he said on a harsh breath when he lifted his mouth from hers. "For our first time together I want us to be in bed. What do you want?"

She nodded. Her body seemed to float as the sexual power of their love took hold of her. "Piers?"

"Yes, darling?"

"There will be regrets, I know there will be."

"And we'll deal with them . . . but not now."

He turned off the water, and they dried each other slowly, eyeing each other in earthly joy.

"You're beautiful."

"You're cute," she said, laughing.

He grinned. "Cute, am I?"

"Yes."

"Sit on this stool, beautiful lady." He took a comb and began working it gently through her damp strands. "You have beautiful hair. I've dreamed of having it coiled around my throat."

"Sounds a little crazy," she murmured, reluctant to talk, reluctant to break the bubble of safety and happiness surrounding her.

"It is." Insanity was wonderful. Damiene was wonderful. She was hot joy, jewellike love, wild, wonderful friendship. How had she managed to have it all?

She reached up to pull his head down and pressed her open lips to his. "Piers."

"Yes?"

"Nothing. Just Piers."

His laugh was shaky, but his hands were firm as they explored her wondrous body.

"I want you," she whispered.

"Me too," he said huskily, and kissed her. Then his mouth left hers and traveled down her body, setting off fires every place it touched.

"Piers!" She wasn't totally without experience, but the velvety sensation of his mouth coursing over her skin was a wild new feeling. He set her aflame, rocketing her beyond orbit to the sexual unknown, the wonder of fantasy becoming reality. What a wild, wonderful adventure! In that moment she unwillingly went through a metamorphosis. The commitment she couldn't give was given. With the joy was a wrenching certainty that no one else would ever command such passion from her.

"Yes, darling." He pulled back from her a fraction, crazy with desire, his breathing harsh with need and want. She was all the woman in the world for him—and that shouldn't have happened. He couldn't love her.

He rose to his feet. "We decided on the bed, didn't we?" At that very moment he wanted her powerfully, but making it perfect for her in every way was of utmost importance. He was damned sure their first time together, wherever it was, would be everlastingly memorable for him.

He swept her up into his arms and carried her out to the hall. "We're very special, my Damiene." And he knew letting her go would be hell.

"What if Miguel returns early?"

"I'll punch his lights out," Piers promised softly. "Stop giggling. Haven't you ever been carried by a naked man before?"

"No." Laughter filled her and she tightened her arms around his neck. She felt amused and aroused, relaxed and tense with desire. Had there ever been such a paradox?

Piers was taken aback at how pleased he was at what she'd told him. No naked man had ever carried her. A pearl of information, at least. A sense of possessiveness invaded him that was entirely new. Damiene had a sophistication that drew him, yet there was something vulnerable and innocent about her that magnetized him more. Why did he want to protect and nurture her? She'd knocked holes in his barriers, penetrated his heat shield, scattered and scrambled his emotions. How?

"What are you thinking?" she asked.

He looked at her and paused at the entrance to his room. "Angel, it isn't just that you've enthralled me. That I could deal with, I guess. How did you manage to make me like it so much and want more?"

"It must be my new perfume. The saleslady said it was a killer."

"Do you shop for expensive perfumes?" He spoke against her mouth.

Breathless, she forgot the question for a moment. "Ah, I shop for samples of expensive perfumes. It protects my budget."

"Good idea." His heart thudded against his ribs.

He was on fire for her, but he couldn't stop the smile that spread over his face. "And you're thrifty too."

"Yes. I learned the value of a dollar at my Scottish grandmother's knee."

He carried her into the room, but didn't put her down right away. Staring at her, he asked hoarsely, "Do you know how many times I've envisioned you in my room?"

"One or two?"

"One or two hundred." He kissed her gently, then placed her on the bed, following her down to lie beside her. The satin coverlet rustled under them.

"My hair is going to make the spread wet," she said.

"I don't care. Do you?"

"This is insane."

"That your hair's wet?" He let his finger trail down from her cleavage to her navel. "Your skin is velvet."

"Thank you. No, I mean the two of us."

"Oh. I like it. Do you?"

"Well, yes, but it's still crazy."

"I like being crazy, then."

It was wonderful to let go, to relax . . . be insane. She stroked his cheek, loving the feel of his skin.

"You're starting a fire, my Damiene, in both of us." He pressed light kisses from her throat to down between her breasts. "Beginning there, I think."

She gripped his head, her eyes closing. "About right."

He gently nipped the soft skin of her belly, his heart pounding when her stomach muscles tightened beneath his mouth. It imitated the contraction of the velvet sheath that would soon surround him.

His hand swept over her, pausing on her silken

thigh, then moving to the hot junction of her body, imbedding itself in the cluster of blond curls there.

When she arched against his hand, he probed deeply into her body, his fingers setting up a fluttering rhythm that spread in waves to her very core.

The feel of her, her heat and moistness, enraptured him. For the first time ever he felt the iron control he'd exercised over all facets of his adult life begin to melt and slip. "Damiene!"

"I want you now," she told him, gazing directly into his eyes.

In gentle fierceness he took her, sliding into her body, gasping with delight when she closed around him, took him as he took her, their passion like a meteor that couldn't be stopped.

"Piers!" Stunned by her own fire, Damiene clung to him as they were swept upward and beyond thought, beyond all sensation except oneness. Her body, mind, and spirit cleaved with his, a joining that was like no other, beyond all expectation, all joy.

Passion was a fire storm that gripped them, spun them, and catapulted them to the stars. Whirling in an ever more powerful force, they could only cling to each other and cry out in ecstasy.

Shuddering in the aftermath, they lay with their arms and legs wrapped around each other, their bodies damp, their hearts still pounding fiercely.

"Damiene?" Piers lifted himself up to look at her.

She smiled, touching his cheek. His eyes were still glazed with receding passion, his hair tousled, his face flushed. "You look a bit piratical," she said softly.

"And you look like Venus, after loving."

She felt the same way, she thought. Never had she

felt so beautiful and desirable, as important as she was at that moment. A new dimension had been added to her, and it was because Piers had loved her, had taken her, had made her new. She'd always been strong before. Now she was all conquering woman because she'd taken love and given it in full measure.

Piers felt as though his entire body were quivering in rebirth. He'd never experienced or imagined such love . . . and he wanted it for all time. There could never be another like Damiene. She was a new sun in his life.

After lovemaking with other women, he had often been eager to be gone, to separate himself from his lover. Now, sighing contentedly, he pulled Damiene close and cuddled her body to his warmth. Closing his eyes, his mouth pressed to her hair, Piers felt an astounding contentment fill him. Happiness was Damiene.

Sleep wrapped them in bliss.

Damiene opened her eyes, then closed them again. She was so at peace and comfortable. There was a warm heaviness on her thigh. When she reached down to it, she encountered Piers's hand. There was no shock, no pulling back, only acceptance. It was so very right being with him, and it stunned her to think she could easily have made love with him at their first meeting because she'd felt the same way then.

A tear slipped from her eye, dampening the pillow. There could be no future with Piers. Already grieving for the time she'd be without him, she moved even closer to him.

He grunted, his hand tightening on her as though he needed her there.

Turning her head, she watched him, his face beautiful in the early morning light. Her heart filled with serenity at the knowledge that life had molded her for this man, that Piers Larraby would pull the sun up in the morning for her, and light the moon to guide her at night.

His eyes opened and he smiled at her. "Now, this I like. Waking up to you is great, lady."

"It's comfy." She was comfortable with him, she mused, as though they'd woken up in each other's arms for years.

Grinning, he kissed her nose. "Comfy? What a slick description of us."

"Isn't it?" She yawned, her hand coming up to her mouth. "Pardon me. My, I feel rested. I can't believe we slept so long, right through dinner.

He chuckled. "Considering your appetite, that is shocking." He laughed as she threw a pillow at him, then captured her in his arms and kissed her soundly. "Are you hungry?"

"Yes," she said tartly, but her eyes were sparkling with laughter. She sat up and started to tell him to hurry up and feed her when she saw his gaze fixed intently on her. She looked down at her bare breasts. "Sorry, I forgot." She drew the covers up to her chin.

"Forgot what?"

"Ah, I'm not sure." Her own gaze was riveted to his wide chest and flat stomach, and a heat was swiftly rising within her. "Oh, Piers."

With his finger he tugged the covers from her grip. Her body was more than beautiful. It was thoroughly sensual—creamy skin and uptilted breasts with the most glorious pale coral nipples. "Stay with me, Damiene, stay with me and be my love. Darling, don't. I didn't mean to make you cry."

She swiped at her cheeks, nodding. "I'm not sad, I'm happy. Really, I am." She leaned down and kissed him gently.

His arms swept around her and he returned her kiss in full measure. It was the first time she had initiated a caress and it made his being balloon with delight.

The magic came immediately. Once more passion swirled through them and they rode out the storm, fused, on fire. Needing and wanting, they gave to each other, until the passion pushed them over the edge and they exploded into the world where only true lovers go.

Piers held her, their uneven breaths brushing across sensitive skin, their bodies pearled with love dew as they descended to earth once more. He pushed his face against her breasts, nuzzling there. "You have a power over me, Damiene Belson."

"You send out some pretty strong signals yourself." She still clung to him, wanting the heat, the euphoric forgetfulness that this man could give her. This was the only man who could call forth such a throbbing, passionate response in her. It was shocking, wonderful, and sad. How long could she keep him, how long could she stay with him? There was no other time, no past, no future. Now was all that counted; being with Piers was the only reality for now.

Pushing aside her somber thoughts, she teasingly punched his arm. "I'm hungry. What about you, Quicksilver Larraby?" He laughed, showing a dimple at one side of his mouth. Damiene hadn't realized until that moment that she loved dimples.

"Let's go." He jumped out of bed, then pulled her up beside him. Looking at her, he winced.

"I hope we're not going to dine like this," she said. She was breathless herself at the sight of his beautiful male body.

"We'd never eat, darling. I want to nibble on you again, right now."

She closed her eyes for a moment, envisioning that. "Sounds pretty good."

"Doesn't it."

Showering together almost sent them back to the bed.

Piers shook his head as he dried off. "I'll dress in the other bedroom, or we'll never eat."

Even after he'd gone, his aura was so strong, Damiene felt she could reach out and touch it. She walked back into his bedroom and looked around the room, reveling in being where Piers slept and spent a great deal of time. She strolled through the room, touching the Chinese lacquered furniture, the jade figurines. She sensed they were valuable. Another clue that Piers was a wealthy man.

She stopped by the bed and her gaze fell on the phone. For days she had been telling herself she should call home and let her parents know where she was. She had been calling about once a week, yet she hadn't spoken to them the whole time she'd been at Piers's. It seemed foolish to call since she didn't have any news about Gilbert's killer. And her parents might ask questions she wouldn't enjoy answering. She wouldn't relish trying to explain Piers to them over the phone.

She turned away from the telephone, knowing she should call. And she would, she promised herself. Tomorrow.

Returning to the bathroom, she dried her hair. Then, wearing a bathrobe of Piers's, she left his suite of rooms and made her way to her own.

Stopping dead on the threshold of her bedroom, she stared at the clothes hanging on the oaken clothes tree. "Charine's," she breathed. She slowly walked into the room and lifted a hand to touch the peach silk pants, the champagne-colored blouse, the red dress.

"Aren't you going to try something on?"

She whirled to face Piers, her eyes stinging with unshed tears. "I can't. It would seem like . . ." She faltered.

He crossed the room and took her in his arms. "Can't you look at it the way it was meant to be? I wanted so badly to buy you something. You're beautiful, darling. They're a gift from a friend who admires and respects you more than anyone he's ever known, man or woman. No other meaning than that."

She looked up at him, one tear rolling down her cheek. "Piers, we've gone too far to turn back. I know that and accept it . . . even if there is no future."

His arms tightened. "Don't talk like that, Damiene. There are obstacles. We knew that going in, but there's no wall high enough to keep me from you. Can't we go on that? Can't we tackle the tough ones when they occur, and enjoy the time we have?"

"That's what we've been doing. Neither looking back or forward."

Her tremulous smile touched him as nothing ever

had. "I don't want you to leave me. How do you feel?"

"I want to stay with you—"

Before she could finish, he kissed her passionately, his hands restlessly stroking her back. A piece of him melted into her at that moment. He was part of her. "You've made me very happy, Damiene."

"Me too." To hell with worry, she thought. She would continue to search for the men who'd killed Gilbert and smeared his name, but she would also share Piers's life as long as possible.

"Hungry?" he asked. "No, wait, that's a stupid question. You're always hungry." He laughed when she cuffed him lightly on the chin. "I hope you realize any touch from you arouses me."

"Oh, no, you don't. You have to feed me."

"Of course." He grinned at her. At least for now she was with him, he thought. They were together. There were still shadows in her eyes that made him want to know who or what had caused them. Putting his questions on hold, he kissed her gently, then led her over to the clothes. "May I choose what you wear?"

Feeling shy, she nodded.

"These." His hand settled on the peach patio pants and camisole top. "You'll drive me crazy, but I want to see you in them. And will you wear your hair down, please?"

She nodded again, her throat too full to speak.

He touched his lips to hers. "Don't be too long, love."

Love! He'd called her love. Damiene stood still long moments after he left, caught in the gentle aura that seemed to surround her whenever Piers was there.

It took more time to dress than she'd planned, because she wanted Piers to approve of her. Never in her life had she felt such longing, such desire to see the fire in a man's eyes.

She lightly applied makeup, and left her long hair free, as he'd requested. Owning only a few pieces of jewelry, she contented herself with buttons of gold in her ears, and nothing on her neck or wrists. The peach silk seemed to change hues when she moved, orange one moment, then delicious apricot. It clung to her body at some places, flaring at others, the lighter-than-air silk totally sensuous.

Leaving the room, she walked quickly toward the kitchen. She could hear Piers whistling a love song. Her heart plummeted and stopped for a moment, then began beating heavily. Piers mesmerized her.

Stopping in the kitchen doorway, she watched him for a moment. He was singing to himself. Happiness bubbled in her because it was so obvious he shared the joy she was experiencing. "Hi."

"Hi." He turned and his eyes widened. "You're wonderful, beautiful."

"Then kiss me." Laughing, she sped across the kitchen and wrapped her arms around his neck.

He obliged her, then lifted his head. "I could forget all about food; dining on you has more appeal."

"I wouldn't mind doing the same to you." One more quick kiss and she pulled back. "But I'm hungry."

He closed his eyes as though in pain. "How can you think of food when we're sharing such a sexy moment?"

"Easy." It was difficult to step back from him, but she could feel her control slipping as it had never done before. Putting on the brakes was a very good idea. Otherwise she'd end up back in his bed. Not that that was such a bad idea. . . .

"Why the dreamy look, Damiene?"

"Just thinking."

"It looked like good thoughts. Were they good?"

"Yes." Staring straight into his eyes, she didn't try to hide her feelings. "Very good."

"Are you sure you wouldn't like to go back to bed? If you keep looking at me that way, we'll be making love in the kitchen."

"Food first." Chuckling, she took his hand and led him to the stove. "What are we having?"

"Plain fare, lady love." He grabbed her and kissed her thoroughly, his tongue probing the sweet inside of her mouth. "You're all the food I need, Damiene."

She clung to him. If only they could truly do what he'd said, shuck their responsibilities and start anew. She wanted that so much.

Five

Several days passed in a haze of joy and ecstasy. Damiene was beginning to believe that she could be with Piers for all time, that their problems would be solved and they would have time to live and love. The thought grew stronger, with each passing hour. Why should she give up the man she loved? Until she found concrete evidence that Gilbert had been murdered, there was no reason to deny herself the comfort and desire she could find with Piers.

That night she and Piers would once again be going to a casino. Each knew the other had greater things to ponder than the turn of a card or the roll of the dice, but the casino provided the type of camouflage they sought, and at the same time let them be together.

No matter how many times Damiene told herself it was business, she couldn't stem the fluttery joy at going out with the man who'd captured her imagination . . . and her heart.

She shouldn't be in love with Piers Larraby, but she was.

That afternoon Piers had gone into Vegas for a meeting, and she told herself it was the perfect time to make the call to her parents that she'd been putting off. She dialed the operator and told her she wanted to reverse the charges. That way it wouldn't appear on Piers's bill.

The phone was answered on the first ring. "Hello."

"Mother, it's me."

"Oh, Damiene, are you all right? We've been worried when you didn't call."

"I'm all right, Mother. I'm sorry I didn't call, but I'm fine. Truly I am."

"Damiene, you must be careful. Our house was vandalized last week when your father and I were at the shop."

Damiene's stomach contracted with fear. "Mother, you and Dad should get out of there."

"No, we won't run, Damiene. Those monsters, whoever they are, have done enough to our family. We're not going to look for trouble, but we won't be intimidated either. Whatever happens, we want you to be safe, dear." Her mother paused. "We might even move to the lake on your return. Your father is convinced the vandalizing has a connection with the people you're looking for."

"I wish I knew who they were."

"Damiene, you sound different to me. Has anything happened?"

"No, Mother." She couldn't tell her mother that a car had chased her, and that her motel room had been ransacked. Or that she'd fallen in love with a gambler. Her mother's pain had made her more fragile, had aged both her parents so much that Damiene wouldn't tell them anything but good news.

"Be careful, dear. You're all we have. I couldn't lose my girl after losing my boy." Her mother's voice broke. "I miss him so much, Damiene."

"We all do, Mother," Damiene answered huskily. Gilbert had been a happy surprise, since her mother had been told she couldn't conceive after Damiene was born. Gilbert had been a joyous addition to the family, adored by parents and older sister, a cheerful baby who'd grown into a delightful young man. Gilbert had been so special.

"Damiene, the police don't feel the vandalizing is connected to Gilbert's death. But we do."

"So do I. Be careful, Mother."

"We will, dear. You do the same."

"I will and I'll keep in touch more regularly."

"Please, we worry so."

"I know. I'm being very cautious."

"I know you have to do this, Damiene, so I won't pester you to come home, but your safety is more important than anything else to us."

"I know, and I'll be careful. You take care of yourself and give my love to Daddy."

"Oh, wait, Damiene, you haven't told me where you're staying. Do you have a telephone number so that I can call if we need you?"

"Ah, yes, I do." She gave her mother the number, then said good-bye. As she hung up, she could feel tears well up in her eyes. Her parents missed Gilbert so much, as did she. How she longed to be home to comfort her mother and father and gain solace from them.

She was so caught up in her memories, she didn't hear the footfalls behind her.

Strong arms encircled her, startling and frightening her. Then relief washed over her when she realized it was Piers, and she winced inwardly at her own reaction. Her life was beginning to revolve around him, and what bemused her was that she was sure there was little she could do to stop that. He had swiftly and smoothly taken over her life.

Her head went back naturally to receive the kisses at the side of her neck. The caresses seemed so right, as though they'd been part of her for a lifetime. "You're early."

"I couldn't stay away." He turned her in his arms, one finger catching a tear. "What happened? Are you all right?" His narrowed gaze scanned the room, then fixed on her once more.

She nodded. "I was thinking about my brother."

"And?"

She hesitated, the habit of keeping her secrets from him momentarily silencing her. But the need to unburden herself to him was too strong.

"He died a couple of months ago of a drug overdose in a motel room in Atlantic City." She swallowed hard. "He wasn't a drinker or a drug user. Even though they couldn't be sure, the police called it an accident."

"Good Lord, I am sorry, darling."

"Thank you. I'm dealing with it better than I did."

"Good." But it bothers you a great deal, doesn't it?" Watching her, he saw her eyes become shuttered. Was her brother the reason she was in Las Vegas?

"Yes," she murmured. "It hurts."

"If I can help in any way, Damiene, I'd like to."

"Thank you." Time to change the subject, she thought. She'd told him enough, and felt the better for it.

Fitting herself more comfortably against him, she looked up at him, twining her arms around his neck. "Did you finish all you set out to do?"

He stared hard at her. She had put him off, and he was certain that meant her brother's death had brought her to Las Vegas. A chill shivered over him. Damiene had no business mixing in something like that.

He kissed her long and hungrily. "Shall we get ready? I thought you might like to have dinner and see a show before we gamble. Does that sound good?"

"Yes." Anything that would put the pitiful sight of Gilbert as she had last seen him from her mind would be a welcome distraction. She and her father had identified his body.

"Will you wear one of your new outfits?"

"All right." She gazed at him warily, something in his expression making her wonder if she'd told him too much. His mind was deep and sharp. Putting two and two together was second nature to him. Well, she would make him forget what she'd said. Tonight belonged to them.

"Maybe I'll wear the cherry-red silk," she said, "How does that sound?" His sudden broad smile rocked her. His pleasure in her choice was obvious.

"Yes, the red. It shouldn't go well with your coloring, but it looks glorious on you."

She tapped him on the nose. "Ah, but there are certain reds that go very well on blondes, the clear ones are good, such as this cherry red."

"Umm, I'm learning." He rested his forehead on hers. "Are you happy?"

"Very."

His heart seemed to soar, knowing she was happy. She was his sunshine. "Why do you sound surprised?" he asked.

"I just never expected this in my life," she said lamely. "I'm not expressing myself very well. . . ."

"You are. I never expected it either, lady love. I never even looked for it." His arms tightened around her. "Lightning struck. I want you."

She chuckled, feeling light as helium. "We're going out. Remember?"

"I remember. But I'd rather stay home and chase you around the house."

The images conjured in her mind had her body flushing with erotic heat. "But Miguel is home this evening. We might shock him."

"I'll pay him to go out, then. I want nothing and no one between us, darling."

"Umm, sounds too good to be true." Staring up at his handsome face, she sighed. "It's all been so fast, so tumultuous from the beginning. Such things have no lasting power. We both know that."

"I don't believe it and neither should you." He brushed some tendrils of hair back from her forehead. "We just shaved some corners, that's all. When destiny calls, you answer or you lose. We answered." He watched a smile grow and fade on her beautiful lips. "Have faith in us, lady."

She shook her head. "We didn't just cut corners, we leapt hurdles and barriers." She brushed her fingers over his cheek. "You're a tough, mysterious guy, Larraby, but you comfort me, and I'll never be able to figure that one out."

"It's easy. We fit together like two halves of a whole." His lips roved up and down her face. "Let's just go with it." His voice was rough, as though there were a barely leashed anger inside him. "All my life I've battled the odds, played the damn game. Now I don't want it in my life. I want only you." He kissed her hard. "And I'm trying to work that one out myself."

"Complex, aren't we? But I think I understand what you're saying. There's so much out there that would interfere with us, that pulls our concentration away from each other."

"And I hate it." Fear for her was a specter that shrouded his happiness with her. "I should have never let you get so close. Yet I want you there."

"Amen to that."

His hard laugh rolled over her. "Damn the world."

Moving back, she stared at him, hungrily taking in every feature, every nuance of expression. "We'll never get out of here.

"Who cares?" He reached for her again, but she avoided his grasp. "Damiene, come here."

"No." She laughed at his scowl. "We're dining out this evening."

"I'd rather dine on you, love."

She closed her eyes for a moment as though pain had touched her. "Don't. Be fair."

He spun on his heel and strode to the door, looking over his shoulder as he crossed the threshold. "I intend to make sure we have more time for the important things, Damiene, like loving. Prepare yourself for that." Then he was gone, the door slamming hard behind him.

Laughter touched with ire spilled from her as she stared at the closed door. He was as frustrated as she by their situation, the secrecy, the other lives they had that constantly intruded. "Was that supposed to intimidate me? I'd love to spend more time with you, Quicksilver Larraby."

Sighing, she turned away and went to the closet for the cherry-red dress.

A dart of pleasure went through her as she slipped the filmy silk tulle over her head. The dress was in an almost starkly simple design, only the material was sophisticated, daring, romantic. The drama of the color and the fabric was subtly sensuous, provocative. Damiene's heart pounded a little faster at the thought of Piers seeing her again in this beautiful dress.

She twisted her hair into a chignon, allowing her long neck to be framed by the collar of the dress. With pearl studs in her ears and her gold watch as her only jewelry, the outfit was devastatingly plain . . . and very rich-looking.

The woman at Charine's had included shoes for her in softest Italian kid, low-heeled and in the same hue as the dress.

Her makeup was the palest cherry-tinted blush, and a hue off the shade of the dress for her lips. Her eyes looked huge when she touched the lids with a pale coral.

Satisfied with her appearance, she headed for the solarium, quite sure she was ahead of Piers.

When she saw him there already, staring out at the desert, a drink in his hand, she stopped.

As though sensing her presence, he turned. His

eyes widened and darkened at the sight of her. He never attempted to hide his desire for her.

Pulses throbbing, she moved toward him. "Well? What do you think?"

"You know what I think, darling."

The husky innuendo in his voice made her gasp. "Yes, I do. Your thoughts border on the illegal, I think."

"Probably." He laughed. "You are devastatingly sexy in that dress, darling. Maybe I should keep you home."

Home, she wondered. It did feel like home living with Piers. She could envision curling up with him on the sofa, with maybe a fire on chilly evenings, his strong arms holding her. After a time he would lift her and carry her to the bedroom and . . .

"Why did you wince? Are the shoes too tight?" Piers studied her face, looked into her eyes, then his smile widened. "Why, Damiene, your thoughts can be as erotic as mine, can't they?"

"You can't read my mind," she retorted.

"Oh, but I can."

She sighed, a smile touching her lips. Then she wrinkled her nose at him. "We should go."

But all she wanted to do was stay. No! She had to focus on her quest. Perhaps tonight she would learn something important. No matter how she might like to shut out the world, she couldn't, not for long anyway. Her parents' pain was her pain. Yet just to put it aside for a short time . . .

"Do you suppose," she asked, "we could pretend for an hour or two that we're simply an ordinary couple out for an evening of dining and gambling?"

"And don't forget dancing," he murmured, sauntering over to her. He could tell that whatever drove her was prickling at her now, yet she wanted forgetfulness, just as he did. At least for a short time.

"Can't forget the dancing," she said softly, feeling the heat of his body as he stopped close to her. "Shall we go?"

"Wouldn't you like a drink first?" He picked a glass of white wine up off a nearby table.

She shook her head.

"Afraid I might have my way with you, wench?"

"Sounds wonderful, but we'd never leave then."

"True. Damiene, will you marry me?"

She stared at him, knowing her mouth was agape. "Piers—"

He held the wineglass to her lips, effectively stopping her words. After she'd sipped, he drank from the same spot. "Don't answer yet, Damiene. Think about it." He kissed the corner of her mouth.

"I don't think I've ever had so much trouble leaving a house." She smiled tremulously.

"You think it's easy for me?" His lips feathered over hers.

She laughed. "Come along, martyr."

He set the wineglass down. "Let's go." She had laughed, he thought, pleased. Maybe for a time she could put aside the specter in her life and dwell on only the two of them.

The Nevada night was clear and warm but with a hint of chilliness in the air. Clouds had been swept away by a puffy breeze that brought the feel of snow in the mountains to the north. Even though it was spring, winter was making a last gesture of defiance.

Damiene studied Piers's profile as they sped through the crystal night. There was so much of him she wanted to commit to memory. Would the time ever come when she couldn't call his face to mind? A sickening sense of loss gripped her. Life's precious moments were few and fleeting.

It seemed to take seconds to reach their destination, though Damiene knew it had taken longer. "The Pink Pearl?"

Piers nodded as he helped her out of the car. "Yes, the food is French and excellent. Then we'll go to Vince's for the floor show and gambling."

She stood next to him as the valet drove away with the car, inhaling the night air and looking around her. "Just for tonight."

Understanding her completely, Piers touched her cheek. "Yes. Just us, just for tonight."

The moment the doorman opened the door, sound assaulted them. Music vied with the calls of the croupiers. "*Faites vos jeux*! Place your bets!" Laughter mixed noisily with the conversations of the crowds.

Damiene held back, hating the violation of the senses. Piers cupped her elbow and urged her forward.

"In the dining room," Piers said in her ear, guiding her toward a tuxedo-clad maître d', "you'll be surprised. The din is barely noticeable. André, this is Miss Belson. Do you have a table for us?"

"Of course." André assessed Damiene discreetly. "Is this a special evening, Monsieur Larraby?"

"We're hoping it will be," Piers murmured, glancing at Damiene.

Heat suffused her at his openly torrid look. "Good evening, André. It's nice to meet you."

"And I'm delighted to meet you, Mademoiselle Belson." André's eyes snapped with curiosity. "You both look very happy."

"We are," Piers said, his smile widening.

"Piers," Damiene said warningly.

The Frenchman smiled. "This evening calls for champagne. Dom Pérignon, of course."

"Not at eighty dollars a bottle," Damiene muttered.

"Mademoiselle Belson, that would be a discount price," André informed her.

"Discount?" Her voice rose in a squeak.

"She's joking," Piers said, taking hold of her upper arm and sweeping into the restaurant. He didn't release her until the maître d' had led them to their table.

Damiene glared at Piers as he took the chair beside hers. "Don't hold back your unholy mirth on my account. Laugh your head off at frugality. See if I care, but when—"

She was interrupted by a waiter's arrival at their table with a silver bucket. He deftly poured a bubbling golden wine into their glasses, bowed, and left. Piers handed her her glass, grinning.

"Why, you . . ." she sputtered. "This *is* Dom Pérignon, isn't it?"

"Just try it, Damiene," he said, struggling to keep from laughing.

After sending him another glare, she sipped her champagne. "Oh, it is good," she admitted. "You're still a monster, though."

He did laugh then, and she smiled reluctantly.

He took her hand. "Why not be my fiancée?"

"Because."

"That's a good reason."

"There are too many to mention."

"I'd like having you as my fiancée. How do you feel?"

"I'd love it, but forget I said that," she said glumly, and sipped more of the delicious wine.

"So would I. Love it, that is." He lifted her hand and pushed a ring on the third finger.

"My Lord, is that an emerald?" she gasped as she tried to pull it from her finger. "It had better be a fake," she muttered, tugging at the beautiful circlet with its green stone.

"It isn't," Piers answered as he managed to keep the ring in place.

"Did you steal it?"

"No."

"Well, that's a comfort." She ceased her battle and held her left hand out in front of her. "It's quite beautiful, isn't it?"

"On your hand, yes." He kissed the ring, then the palm of her hand.

Damiene felt as though tiny birds were fluttering in her stomach. She'd never felt so helpless, so vulnerable . . . so strong.

Dinner was lobster flown in from Maine, with lyonnaise potatoes and Caesar salad.

"Not all French, but all fabulous," she said, inhaling the luscious odors.

"*Nouvelle*," Piers said, smiling. "But they prepare the seafood as they do in Marseille. No one has the reverence for food that the French do."

They lingered over fruit and cheese and demitasse, then left the restaurant.

"Won't your friend Vince be miffed that you didn't choose his place?" Damiene asked languidly, leaning on his arm as they strolled along the Strip.

Piers shrugged, kissing her hair. "He knows I have varied tastes in food."

"Oh."

Noting her preoccupation, he glanced at her, following her gaze as they approached Vince's. "You're remembering when we met, aren't you?"

She looked up at him. "Wild, huh?"

He saw how her smile wobbled. "Yes, but I wouldn't change anything if it meant we'd never have met."

She reached up and kissed him on the mouth.

Watching them together caused the knot of hatred to tighten in his gut. Getting rid of Piers Larraby would go a long way to alleviating that discomfort, and it looked like getting rid of Miss Belson at the same time would be a bonus.

Piers abruptly broke the kiss, lifting his head and looking around.

"What is it?" Damiene asked.

"I don't know. A funny feeling." It was the same feeling he'd had at his casino in London the night his partner had been killed. "Let's go inside."

Hurrying Damiene in front of him, he shot quick glances over his shoulder. He couldn't see anyone suspicious on the crowded street. But that didn't mean anything, He'd learned, long ago, to pay attention to his hunches.

Damiene turned to face him when they were in the large gold and diamanté decorated foyer. "You saw something."

"No, love, I didn't. I told you the truth. I had a strange sensation."

"That someone was watching you?"

"Yes."

"I know the feeling."

Putting his arm around her, he ushered her into the premier gambling room. He looked down the long corridor toward Vince's office and saw his friend standing several feet away, talking with one of the dealers. Piers smiled, relaxing somewhat.

"You've known him a long time, haven't you?" Damiene asked.

"Yes. His brother Berto and I were . . . good friends for years. Berto was killed in a fire in London two years ago." Piers halted, wondering how much to tell her. Then he remembered how she had opened up to him by telling him about her brother's death. Perhaps it was his turn to open up.

"Actually," he went on, "Berto and I were business partners. We owned a casino in London. The night he died, I had left him there after we closed. He said he wanted to go over some figures again. He had a suspicion someone was skimming money." Piers's voice was bleak. "I hadn't been gone five minutes when the club exploded. The police surmise that we had an enemy who'd bombed the place."

He shook his head. "I still miss him. He was a good man, and a good friend. One of the best I've ever known."

Damiene squeezed his hand, wishing she could chase away the sadness in his eyes. "I'm so sorry, Piers. It's strange, though, isn't it? Both of us losing a dear one." That her life and Piers's could run on such parallel lines was weird indeed. She shivered.

He put his arm around her. "Yes." Seeing her pensive expression, he leaned down and kissed her hard. "Think of me and what we have, darling. Remember? Just for tonight."

"Yes." She smiled at him, then turned to face Vince, who had finished his talk with the dealer and was approaching. "Hello, Vince."

"Hello, Damiene. How are you? Piers." Vince slapped his friend on the back. "Sit down, man. Have you eaten? Going to have a drink before you gamble?"

"I thought we might. Damiene, what would you like?"

"A sunburst, please. That's—"

"I know," Vince said. "Sparkling mineral water and orange juice with a twist of lime."

"I'll have a Scotch and soda," Piers said.

Vince gave their order to a cocktail waitress while Piers seated Damiene at a small table in the lounge area above the gambling floor.

"I'll join you," Vince said when their drinks arrived.

"What is it?" Piers asked. "You look tired."

"I had a call a few days ago, inquiring about Damiene—" Vince didn't wince when Piers gripped his arm. "I knew you'd be upset. And if I'd been able to get more information from the caller, I would've gotten in touch with you at once. The moment I asked a question the connection was broken."

"Tell me everything they said. Was the voice male or female?" Piers took hold of Damiene's hand.

Vince's gaze flickered over their clasped hands, and a small smile played around his mouth. "I would say male, but I'm not sure. The voice was muffled. Whoever it was asked for Miss Belson." When I said she wasn't here, he or she asked if she worked for me and did I know where she lived."

"Damn! How could they connect her with you?"

"I thought about that and I think I have it. I took two of my men with me when I went to that motel and collected her things. Then I paid her bill. The motel man called me by name."

Piers spat an epithet. "You're too damned well known in this town." He turned to Damiene for the first time, and cursed under his breath at her pallor. "You don't have anything to fear, Damiene."

"I should get away from you," she said, her eyes wide as she stared at him. Piers was in danger, she was certain of it.

"No!" he said fiercely.

Head turned at nearby tables.

"Easy, man," Vince said gently, patting Piers on the arm.

"Maybe we should go home," Piers muttered.

"We were going to gamble," Damiene said. "Right?"

"Yes, dammit," he said quietly, his smile hard.

"Tough as old boots, isn't he, Damiene?" Vince said.

She smiled faintly. "Yes."

Vince shrugged when Piers glared at him. "Only telling the truth."

"Damiene doesn't need any more ammunition, thank you," Piers said curtly, eliciting a laugh from his friend. "What do you hear from Bear and Dolph?"

Vince chuckled. "Well, for one thing, neither one of them wanted to disturb you."

Damiene could feel her face flame.

"Dammit, Vince, Damiene isn't one of the boys. Don't make remarks like that in front of her."

"Piers, you sound positively priggish," Damiene said.

"He's right." Vince smiled. "Sometimes I forget

myself when I'm with the three of them, or even talking about them. I apologize for my wayward tongue, Damiene."

She smiled in acknowledgment. "Are you with them often?"

"Not as much as we used to be. Since my brother's death, neither Piers nor I care to go to London very often, which is where we all used to meet regularly. And now that Piers spends so much time on his guest—"

"No need to go into that," Piers interrupted sharply.

"Sorry," Vince said. "I assumed she knew."

"She doesn't. Damiene and I have a cardinal rule about not discussing everything in our lives with each other."

Damiene swallowed a sigh. How eager she was to hear any morsel about his life, something she'd have to savor and dream over when they were no longer together.

Piers recognized the disappointment and frustration on her face. He felt that way about her, too, and all they could share with each other. But he didn't want her to know that the police who investigated the club fire had told him he might be in danger too. As if it were right in front of him, he saw again the car that had almost hit Damiene the night they met. Cold sweat beaded his body. Sitting straight in his chair, he stared at Vince.

"What is it, Piers?" he asked. "Damn, you look like someone dumped you into an open grave and was shoveling the dirt over you."

"What if the car that chased us down the night I met Damiene wasn't after her but me? What if *I* was the target." He sat back in his chair, drumming his fingers on the table.

"That can't be, Piers," Damiene said haltingly. "The car was already chasing me when you first saw me."

"There could be reasons for that too," he said. What if it had all been a setup?

"What are you thinking?" she whispered.

"Maybe it would be a good idea if you moved into town just as you suggested. I could find—"

"No! I'm not leaving if you're in danger. You wouldn't let me leave when you thought I was threatened, so I'm not leaving now, either."

"Dammit, it's my house."

"Then throw me out."

Vince laughed, then tried to smother it with his hand when Piers glared at him. "I think she's almost as tough as you, Piers."

"Tougher." Piers exhaled sharply. "Let's gamble." He lifted Damiene's hand to his mouth and kissed it. "I'll keep you safe."

"I believe you."

A sharp pain shot through his chest when she smiled. She had taken over his life and he didn't want her out of it now. For the first time in years he felt true fear. His former reckless plunging into risks now took on a macabre, distasteful tinge. He would continue his quest, but with prudence. No more tumbling into dangerous situations and somehow working his way out. Tight planning would be the order of the day. Protecting Damiene would be paramount.

They made their way through the room, Damiene saying she wanted to start with blackjack. When they reached a table, she glanced at him. "Playing baccarat?"

"No. Tonight I have a hankering to watch you play cards . . . maybe even play against you."

"I'll beat you."

"Would you like to place a small wager on the outcome?" he asked lazily.

"Of course." She grinned at him, excitement rising in her at the heat in his smile.

It would be good, he thought, to put the fear on hold.

Six

Watching the woman play blackjack was eye-opening. Her skill was a surprise. Carefully, thinking out her card choices, she won more than she lost. A time or two she went over the top with a couple of good moves. She was daring but calculating. Obviously her sweet face hid a steel-trap mind. She and Larraby were quite a combination. What would they say if they knew their enemy was in the casino with them?

Damiene looked around when she felt someone standing at her back. she smiled, seeing it was Vince. "Am I winning too much?" she asked softly. "I could feel you watching me."

He stiffened. "You could feel me watching you? I was over in the cashier's cage, Damiene, counting receipts."

"Oh? It must have been someone else, then."

"Yes, I'm sure. Excuse me, will you." He strolled around to the other side of the table, where Piers was sitting, and bent down and whispered to him.

Piers eased to his feet, glancing left and right, his manner relaxed. But his eyes glittered obsidian, dangerous.

Damiene lost a close one with the dealer and looked up at Piers, a rueful smile on her face. He was gone!

"Are you playing, madame?" the dealer asked.

"Ah, no, I'm out this round. Thank you." Rising quickly, she looked about. Maybe Piers had gone to Vince's office. Unsure what to do, she headed for the ladies' room, hoping Piers would be back when she returned.

Piers made a circuit of the room, staying within sight of the blackjack table. But when he glanced back to where Damiene was sitting, she was gone. Damn! Where did she go? His gaze flicked quickly from table to table. Ladies' room!

Striding along the parquet area that surrounded the gaming room, he quickly reached the ladies' room. He paused in front of the door, then pushed it open and entered.

"Wrong one, fella. Can't you read?" A glossy brunette looked him over from head to foot. "Nice."

"Excuse me." He moved past her. "Damiene? Are you in there?" He ignored the gaping towel woman, who was the only other occupant of the ornate wash area.

"Piers?" Damiene strode into the wash area, glaring at him. "I thought I must be hearing things. Get out of here! This is— "

"I know where I am. Are you ready?"

"I want to wash my hands. Will you leave?"

"When you're ready." He took a towel from the still-shocked attendant and shoved a couple of bills at her. "Here."

"Vince will ban you from his casino and I don't blame him." She smiled weakly at the attendant, who gazed from the cash in her hand to the madman in her ladies' room.

"A man!" an older woman exclaimed as she opened the door. "Pervert!" She quickly backed out.

"Let's get out of here," Piers said, his taut expression relaxing into a lopsided grin as she laughed helplessly.

"You're crazy . . ." Damiene's mirth faded. "But then again, maybe you're not."

They left the ladies' room and she stopped a few paces beyond the door. "Something happened. What?"

"Nothing, as far as I know. Vince said that you felt someone was watching you. Is that right?"

His jaw was clenched, and his hands were balled into fists. "Piers? Look at me. It's all right. I just made a mistake. It happens."

He gazed down at her, seeing the hidden areas she tried to hide. "You did feel someone was watching you, though, didn't you?"

"Yes." She couldn't lie to him.

"I want you to stay with me." His arm encircled her waist, fixing her to his side. "Let's dance. Vince has the best jazz band in the city." He wanted to hold her forever, keep her safe, run from the world and take her with him.

He led her onto the dance floor. Putting his arms around her, he pressed his mouth to her hair, closing his eyes, inhaling the wonderful special essence that was Damiene. For a little while he could dwell in Eden . . . but he was certain the time was coming when he would have to separate from her to protect her. You couldn't do all the probing and digging he'd done and not make someone uneasy, and finally wrathful enough to take action. Soon he'd have to part from Damiene. But first he'd find the people who were threatening her and take care of that. Once she was safe . . .

"Hey, what planet are you on?" Damiene eased back from him a little, studying him. "You're not still dwelling on what happened at the table, are you?"

"No, but it does bring back the incontrovertible fact that someone has been trying to get at you since your arrival in Las Vegas."

And maybe they'd struck before, she thought. She'd never believed the crash that had killed Gilbert's friends, the ones he had gone to Atlantic City with, had been an accident. A few days after Gilbert's funeral, one of them had called her. He told her her suspicions that Gilbert had been murdered were correct, and he was sure he knew who the murderer was. A man named Barnaby Echo.

When she asked him how he knew this, he became flustered and stammered out that Gilbert had been in the wrong place at the wrong time.

She tried to find out more, who Barnaby Echo was and how Gilbert's friends knew him, but her questions panicked him. He told her he was sorry and hung up. Two days later he and the other two young men who'd been in Atlantic City were killed in a hit-and-run car accident.

"I think both of us need to come down from strange worlds," Piers whispered into her ear.

Startled, she gazed up at him. "Right." He tightened his hold and she closed her eyes and snuggled closer. "Nice."

"Umm."

The music was good, jazzy, hot, slow, sweet . . . and fast.

The rhythm changed and Piers let her swing free of his body.

Laughing with sudden joy, Damiene let her soul dictate the dance.

Neither noticed the hard-bitten casinogoers who suddenly smiled, watching them, as though memory had softened and sent a wonderful personal message to them.

When the music changed again and she was close to Piers's chest, Damiene sighed.

"Tired?" he asked.

"No. Replete. I haven't done this in so long."

Piers didn't miss the poignancy in her tone. "Well, why don't we make up our minds to do it twice a week. How does that sound?"

"Like a commitment," she said ruefully.

"And you don't think we can do that."

She shook her head. "Our lives are filled with secrets, we both know that . . . and we have things to do."

"So we have," he said softly, his cheek pressed against her hair. "Why not take one day at a time, make plans . . . and maybe they'll work out. Couldn't hurt."

It would hurt like hell when she had to leave him. "Right. What could it hurt?"

He felt the almost infinitesimal shudder go through her body. He kissed her hair.

They danced until the casino was emptying of people and dawn was closer than midnight.

Piers was loath to release her when the music finally stopped. There would be a late cabaret, but the dance music was done. "Shall we go?" he whispered huskily.

Damiene nodded without speaking, wanting those strong arms around her forever.

Piers was helping Damiene with her wrap when Vince approached them, his eyes red-rimmed. Piers shook his head. "You need some sleep, chum. Why not let someone else do the counting and you go to bed?"

Vince shrugged. "Maybe I will. But remember, Berto always said that a man should handle his business, not give it over to others."

Piers nodded.

Damiene noticed the pensive look on both faces, as though they could call the departed Berto to mind with ease. She squeezed Piers's hand. "You still miss him, don't you?"

"Oh, yes." He blinked away the memory and smiled down at her. "But that's one of the blessings of coming to Vince's. We often speak of Berto and the many things he said and did."

"Or if you're with Bear and Dolph you talk of him," Vince said. "They liked him too."

Piers nodded. "They did. And they feel as we do about apprehending his assassin."

"That's your quest," Damiene said slowly. "Your secret."

"Yes." He gazed into troubled eyes. "It's not vengeance, darling, it's justice."

"And how often have the two been transposed?" she murmured, thinking of her own quest. "What if," she continued, almost to herself, "it becomes destructive, not constructive?"

"I've come too far to turn back," Piers said hoarsely.

She nodded. "I know the feeling."

"Damiene—"

She put her fingers across his lips, loving the instant caress of that tough mouth. "I understand, truly I do." Her gaze moved to Vince. "I don't mean to denigrate your brother's memory."

"I know." Vince smiled.

"He sounds like a wonderful person."

"You would have liked him, darling. He was always laughing or singing, or both." Piers gazed at her searchingly, relieved that she wasn't pursuing her previous line of thought.

Vince chuckled. "And he didn't always sing in tune."

Piers smiled. "And you used to tell him that too."

Damiene watched the two men, smiling to mask her own turmoil. She was amazed that she and Piers shared the same quest. So why should she question his actions when her own were fashioned from the same fabric? Was Piers's search for vengeance but a reflection of her own? Looking into the mirror was painful. Wasn't her search for the men who'd ruined Gilbert's life much the same as Piers's quest?

Was it healthy to put aside living, for a hunt? Were such actions ultimately destructive to the hunter? She looked at each man in turn. There could be no doubt that both were deeply bereft, that

Berto had been important to them. Yet, had the search become more important than the person? Discordant emotions soured her stomach and she shook her head to clear it of unwanted thoughts.

"Are you ready to go?" Piers asked her.

"Yes. Good night, Vince, and thank you for my winnings."

Piers chuckled. "I don't think two hundred dollars is considered a killing, darling."

"Maybe not to you, but it shows I'm improving. Why, in all the casinos I've been . . . " Her voice trailed off.

Noting the rise of color in her cheeks, Piers shook his friend's hand and ushered her from the casino. They strolled back to The Pink Pearl and waited for the car to be brought around.

Piers slipped his arm around her waist. "You don't have to fear giving away any information to me, darling."

She looked up, her smile wry. "Habit, I suppose. I've hidden my moves so long that when I do say something, I feel instantly defensive." And now she could admit to a growing feeling of discontent with her life. Oh, she still wanted the men who'd wronged her brother to be brought to justice. But being with Piers had brought home most fearfully the knowledge that life was a fleeting thing, that beauty was easily lost, never to be regained, that it was better to go for the gold than the dross. Vengeance was dross; Piers was gold.

When the car arrived, Piers handed her in, then went around and got in the driver's side. Taking her hand, he kissed it gently. "We both have too many cloudy corners in our life, but that won't get in the way of what we have. I won't let it."

"There might be too many things we can't put aside, Piers."

"No! Don't get caught up in that, Damiene. There's room in my life for you, and I'm damn sure there's room in yours for me." He engaged the gears and pulled away with a squeal of tires, careering out into the street, turning the heads of some of the late-nighters.

"Going to crash the car?' she asked, placing her hand over his as it gripped the wheel.

He turned his hand into hers. "Whatever it takes to make you see that we belong together."

"I don't need convincing, Piers, I thought you knew that. It's the circumstances that are dictating the policy, not my feelings or yours."

"We'll change that."

Laughter bubbled through her, and for a moment the tension was put on the shelf. "Biiig man."

An ironic smile touched his mouth. "Yeah, that's me. But I mean it, darling. I'll fight it out with anyone to keep us together."

"How arousing," she said huskily, batting her eyes at him.

"You might think you're being funny, but you are arousing me, my sweet."

"That's probably the easiest task on the planet."

"For you it is."

"You say the darnedest things." She tried to glare at him when he chuckled, but she couldn't keep the smile from her face. It was so easy to be seduced into the tranquility that was Piers's special aura, at least for her. How was he able to give her such contentment in the midst of chaos? She swallowed a sigh. And her life was chaotic, no doubt about it.

"Relax," he told her. "There's just the two of us, and that's what's important."

"Yes." She leaned her head against the back of the seat. "Would you mind if I called my family tomorrow? I want—"

"There's no need to request that from me," he said abruptly. "I think of the house as our home."

Her heart plunged to her shoes, then shot up to her throat in one delightful millisecond. "Thank you."

He shot her a quick look. "Don't you think of it as home?"

She nodded.

"Thank you, darling. You've made me very happy."

"You make me happy."

He took her hand and lifted it to his mouth, his tongue scorching her palm, following the lifeline.

Damiene didn't remember getting out of the car when they arrived at the house. All her focus was on Piers and the wonderful closeness they shared.

Walking through the house was like a homecoming, but the serenity was charged, their bodies throwing off enough sparks to set the desert grass on fire. Desire was a flame that licked through them, melted them together.

"Could we swim?" Damiene whispered.

"Yes." Blood thundered through him. He wanted her with an elemental need he'd known only with Damiene, never before with anything or anyone else. He could have exploded with desire, yet he wanted to cherish and care for her as though she were the most precious thing on earth. She was!

She started to turn toward her room, but he tugged her back. "I thought I'd get my suit," she said.

"You don't need one, darling."

She gasped and stared up at him. His features were silvered by the low beam of the night-light in the hall. "Devil." She put her hand up to caress his beautiful mouth as she moved closer to her.

"I want to see you in the water," he murmured against her neck, "gaze at your creamy skin and your sexy curves." He pulled back. "What do you want?"

"The same," she said breathlessly. "Oh, Piers, is this real?"

"More than real, love. This is right, the way it should be." He lifted her into his arms and carried her through to the solarium. "Miguel had better be in bed."

Damiene chuckled. "He'll probably quit."

"Let him," Piers said carelessly. "I want you, my darling. No one else."

When they reached the solarium, he let her slide down his body. "Shall I undress you?"

"No. We'd never get out of the dressing room."

"True. Hurry." He watched her until she disappeared into a cubicle, then hurried into another one, stripping off his tie and shirt, scattering his clothes every which way.

When Damiene reappeared she was wrapped in a towel. She spotted Piers at once, swimming a slow breaststroke, his strong body partially veiled by the rippling water.

Going to the side of the pool, she dropped the towel.

Piers stopped swimming at once, his gaze going over her slowly. "You're too beautiful, Damiene Belson," he told her huskily.

"Thank you." Poising for a moment, she brought her arms up over her head, consciously seductive.

She felt beautiful at that moment, lissome, desirable. Pies did that!

Rising on her toes, she sprang from the side of the pool, entering the water cleanly. Piers grabbed her instantly, then his mouth was on hers and they rose to the surface slowly, holding each other, their lips parted, their tongues seeking, wanting.

Holding her, Piers glided to the side of the pool and maneuvered her over his aroused form. "Umm, you feel good, lady."

"So do you." She closed her eyes. So, this was ecstasy.

"Damiene, I love you."

She caught her breath as excitement bubbled in her. There was tenderness and loving, too, all for Piers. He'd taken her world, a world that bordered on the insane, and smoothed it out with gentleness, concern, and a passion she hadn't even dreamed existed.

"I never expected to find you, darling," he said and undulated his body beneath hers, sending water lapping over her.

Gasping with pleasure, she gripped his shoulders and closed her eyes. "We shouldn't love each other."

"Do you love me, Damiene?"

"Yes, I do." Clasping her legs around his waist, she pushed down, loving Piers's hoarse exhalations, his passionate grip on her body.

"No! Damiene, darling, stop. It's too soon for you."

"No! No, it isn't."

Mushrooming out of control, their passion captured them and sealed them together in a cascade of joy and love.

"You're mine."

"I love you, Piers."

Holding each other, they came back to earth, panting, enthralled . . . and committed.

"That's so wonderful," she murmured. "Do you suppose there's a patent on it?" She felt dizzy, powerful, almighty.

"How could there be? We just discovered it." He kissed her cheek, her eyes, the stream of wet hair. "Marry me right away."

She pushed back from him, blinking. "What? What did you say?"

"I think you heard me."

She glanced away. "It's lovely to think on, as my Irish grandmother would say, but . . . we know it's a pipe dream, don't we, Piers?"

He frowned. "Come on. Let's get into the hot tub before we get chilled."

"I haven't even swum yet," she said shakily.

"You can do that after you're warm."

He vaulted out of the pool, then reached down to catch her under the arms and lift her from the water. At the hot tub, he pressed the button to start the mechanism, then led her down into the hot, steaming, swirling water.

"There," he said. "How's that?"

"Fine, this is wonderful."

"Great. Now tell me why you won't marry me right away."

"Oh, Piers, you can see how foolish it would be to make plans when we're both caught up in other things."

"I don't see that. I think we have some things to settle and work through, problems in our lives that have to be handled. But it won't always be that way. I want you as my wife. What do you want?"

"The same." Tears clouded her eyes, and he pulled her close. "I'd like nothing better than to plan a wedding with you."

"Then let's do it. Plan a wedding, I mean. Along the way there'll be interruptions . . . but things could settle themselves, too, for both of us."

"That's reaching," she muttered. But hope, refusing to be tamped down, bubbled in her. "Piers, hasn't it occurred to you that neither of us has completely opened up to the other about what the problem is in our lives? That we're talking about the ultimate intimacy with secrets still between us?"

"I'm aware of that. Take a chance on us, Damiene, and then we'll talk about our problems and what we can do."

"Marry you," she said dreamily, snuggling closer, sitting on his lap.

"This is not the way to carry on a serious conversation." Piers exhaled shakily, his eyes closing as she pressed her mouth to his ear. "You are arousing me, darling."

"Only fair, since you're doing the same to me." She wriggled her backside against him.

The water roiled like a mini tidal wave as Piers took her hard and fast, eliciting cries of excitement from her.

They exploded again in a passioned joining that stopped the world and tumbled them into the magic that only lovers know.

"Oh, Piers." Her arms tightened around his neck. "Yes."

"Yes, darling, it was wonderful."

"It was. But I was giving you an answer to your proposal."

He held her away from him to stare at her, then pulled her close again and kissed her thoroughly.

Giddy, she ran her hands over his face. "I'm going to savor this moment, Piers. I want to hold it and look at it and keep it forever."

"We will, darling. There are years for us, not just moments." If it took a lifetime, he would wipe the shadows from her eyes.

"Piers," she said, cuddling close to him. "I want to tell you about my brother. He was the apple of my parents' eye. We all loved him. He was the sunshine in the family. My parents have been trying to put his death in perspective, but it's taken its toll." She shook her head. "I've hoped that finding out more about what happened would help them."

"And that's why you're here in Las Vegas?"

She nodded. "Gilbert was killed in Atlantic City. He didn't gamble, but he worked with a group of people who took junkets to gambling areas a few times a year. He'd never gone before, but two months ago he did and . . ."

"He lost his life."

"Yes." She shook her head. "None of his friends knew he was missing. Or so they said. They thought he'd gone back to his room, because he hadn't won much and he wasn't that interested in gambling. The next morning when everyone was ready to head for the airport, he didn't answer a knock at his door. When the manager opened his room, they found him dead, an overdose. Gilbert had never used drugs."

Piers hugged her, seeing the grief in her eyes, the puzzlement and the anger.

"He was so gentle. Every dog and cat in the neighborhood found their way to our house because Gilbert would feed them. We had a garage full of strays, the sick ones in cages, the others just hanging around, some in the house even." She gave a watery chuckle. "Mother would get exasperated, especially when one exuberant retriever Gilbert had found stood up at her counter and ate an entire rice pudding, hot from the oven. Gilbert got accepted to veterinary school at Cornell University and he'd been working full-time to save as much money as he could. My parents almost had to force him to accompany his friends. They knew he needed a break."

"And now they have regrets along with the grief?"

"Oh, yes, so many regrets." Tears glistened in her eyes when she looked at him.

Piers's heart squeezed with anguish for her. "And you're trying to assuage some of that by finding the people responsible for his death."

"Yes!"

"I'll help you any way I can, I mean that."

"I can't say I have a hot trail since I have only one name. I finally found someone in Atlantic City who'd heard of him, and he told me he was in Las Vegas. That's what brought me here. I'm looking for Barnaby Echo."

"Barnaby Echo. Never heard of him. Strange name, I think I'd remember if I'd ever heard it. I'll ask around. There's sure to be someone who would recall such an unusual name." He caught her gesture when she tried to mask a yawn. "Come on, love. It's bedtime. I'll tell you my story another time."

She nodded, yawning hugely. "I am sleepy."

"Maybe it's from unburdening your soul and some of the tension melting." He kissed the top of her head as he helped her from the hot tub, then wrapped a warmed bath sheet around her. "Let's go to bed."

They walked slowly down the hall to the master suite, arms around each other. Once in the bedroom, it took them only seconds to slide between the satin sheets.

"I wish we weren't going to sleep," Damiene said drowsily, then her eyes closed. Sleep wrapped her like a down quilt.

Piers held her in his arms and stared up at the darkened ceiling. If it took all he had, he'd find Gilbert's killer for her. She didn't have to tell him that her quest had taken its toll of her, not just of her mother and father. It was in her speech patterns, the dark spaces in her eyes, the almost invisible tic at the corner of her mouth when she spoke of her beloved brother. And she would never quit until it was resolved. So, he would take a hand. Having a life with Damiene had become all-important. Even his own search had slipped to the back shelf of his mind. Damiene was premiere. Nothing else took precedence.

Seven

"And you've heard the name Barnaby Echo, Dolph?" Piers asked, his hand tightening around the phone. That was why he had made this conference call to them first thing that morning. "I should have known your photographic memory would remember something."

"The problem is," Dolph said, "I can't recall in what context I heard it, where or when. I'll have to cogitate."

Bear chuckled. "Going to hide out in a monastery?"

"That'll be the day," Piers said.

"Guffaw, if you must, gentlemen."

"Listen, you two," Piers said, serious again, "I need to know how that name is connected to Gilbert Belson. My lady is sickening because of what happened to her brother. I can't have that."

"She is one special person," Bear said quietly. "I could see that."

"Yes," Dolph said. "She's quality . . . and you love her, Piers."

"She's everything," he said simply.

"I think I envy you, Piers," Bear said. "I can't see that ever happening to me."

"Nor to me," Dolph added.

"I never expected Damiene myself," Piers said.

"We'll find Barnaby Echo, whoever he is," Bear promised.

"Could it be a company?" Dolph wondered out loud. "Some sort of novelty place?"

"Remembering something?" Piers asked, sitting forward in his chair.

"Not really. Just a thought, nothing concrete. But the name is strange enough to be a novelty title of some kind. Damn! Why is it familiar to me? Was it a film? The name of a character in a play? Don't know. Hopefully it'll come to me."

"We'll shake the bushes every way we can," Bear said. "We'll uncover something. Are you going to ask Vince?"

Piers hesitated. "I trust him, no doubt of that, but I think I'll leave him out of this unless we really need him. I regret involving him in some of my investigations about Berto's death."

"I know what you mean," Dolph said. "He can still get very upset when we talk of Berto, yet he encourages us to speak of him."

"Damn the persons who killed old Berto," Bear said huskily.

"Yes," Piers said. "And I haven't been able to pick up any solid leads there in some time. Neither has Vince." His fingers clenched on the pencil in his hand, breaking it in two jagged pieces. "It's as though everything went up in smoke."

"Has it occurred to you," Bear asked, "that the culprits have gone to ground because they know we're after them? Maybe the rest of us might be patient with them if we corralled them . . . but Vince would kill them. They might know that."

"You've got a point, Bear. It doesn't make it easier to take though."

"Be patient, Piers," Dolph said. "We found Irmy Wilbur with those marked bills on him."

"Yeah, but he was dead," Bear said disgruntledly. "Berto and his hunches!"

Piers sat back in his chair, rubbing his forehead. "If Berto hadn't thought to mark some bills because he was suspicious of skimming, we might never have found out about Wilbur."

"But we still don't know if there's a connection there with Berto's death."

"But it's a lead, Bear," Dolph said. "And we'll connect some of the dots pretty soon, I feel it."

"Good," Piers said sharply. "But first I want to get this thing cleared up for my lady."

"We'll do it," Bear said. "Where is she?"

"She's still sleeping. Totally exhausted."

"I hear the worry in your voice, Piers," Dolph said, "and I don't blame you. But don't unravel. We'll get the suckers who caused her all this grief. Bet your check on it."

"I already have," Piers murmured. "Keep in touch."

"Always."

"You bet."

When the connection was broken, Piers stared at the phone for long seconds. Would he and his friends be able to hunt down the people who'd killed Gilbert? Why had he been killed? Why kill a person who'd made no big score at the tables? A connection from gambling to a veterinary student seemed outlandish. The kid had had minimal money, yet his death, from Damiene's description, had all the earmarks of a drug dealer's hit. What would the mob have on Gilbert Belson?

On impulse he called Vince. "It's Piers. Vince, do you still have that list of dealers and croupiers, countrywide? Worldwide? I didn't realize that. Is it like a union list? I want to look up a name if I could. No, I don't want you to do it." He held the receiver away from his ear. "All right, all right, so I was wrong. I shouldn't spare you if it's about Berto. And I won't anymore. But this has to do with Damiene and I don't—" Again he held the receiver away, wincing at the tirade. "Fine. I'm wrong again. But listen, Bear, Dolph, and I thought—no! don't start again. We won't keep anything from you. Calm down, will you. You'll scare your customers."

Piers inhaled and sank deeper into the leather desk chair. "Damiene has been searching for a man who could be responsible for her brother's death." In terse sentences Piers sketched what he knew of Damiene's brother and his death. "And all she knows is the name of one person. Barnaby Echo. Know him? It is a strange name, but I've never heard it either. Will you look it up in that list you have? Thanks. Talk to you soon."

Piers hung up the phone, then stood and stretched, yawning. When he heard a knock on the door, he called, "Come in."

Damiene opened the door and stood hesitantly on

the threshold. She'd never been in his study before. "Good morning. Am I interrupting something?"

"Not at all." He crossed the room to her, pulling her into his arms for a long, loving kiss. "I was just talking to Vince. And before that I'd been talking to Bear and Dolph." He touched her cheek gently. "They want to help find Barnaby Echo."

Startled, she stared at him.

"Not to worry, love, they'll be discreet."

"I was thinking that it might be dangerous for them. If someone would shoot up Gilbert with drugs for no good reason, think what they could do if someone threatened them."

More than once Piers had thought that about Damiene's involvement, but he knew better than to try to dissuade her. Keeping his arm around her, he led her from the study to the kitchen. "Let's get some breakfast. No need to worry about Dolph and Bear. They're carved out of steel. No tougher men ever lived."

When they entered the kitchen, Miguel glanced at them and smiled, revealing his missing eye tooth.

"What's for breakfast?" Piers asked. He reached for an orange and began peeling it.

Miguel shrugged. "Whatever you like. Juice, eggs, ham, biscuits—"

"Oatmeal," Damiene pronounced firmly. Both men looked at her. "Yes, it's time I was back on my health foods again. I've been eating hit and miss for too long. I crave foods without additives or cholesterol." She laughed.

"Wow. Sounds like a nutrition high." Piers grinned at her, delighted to see her smile, loving the dimples at the corners of her mouth.

"Wait," she said. "I think I'll run first, then come back for breakfast."

Miguel's smile widened. "Maybe you can beat the Fatback here. He hasn't been keeping in shape."

"Shut up, Miguel," Piers said mildly. "I'll have oatmeal too. And we'll see who can run."

"If you can't carry him home, Damiene," Miguel said, "call a freight outfit. They'll handle it."

"I should break your neck," Piers muttered.

"Any time."

"How about right—"

Damiene whirled and left the kitchen. "I'm going for my run now. See ya."

"Damiene! Wait."

"Better get the lead out, Piers."

"I'll talk to you later, Miguel."

Piers raced after her, calling to her when she took over the bathroom in the master suite. He heard her laugh, and happiness built in him like a flood. "Hurry up or I'll leave you in the dust," she said.

"That'll be the day."

He grabbed his sweats and running shoes and in minutes was out of his room. He saw Damiene head out the front door, moments ahead of him. Then he was after her, sprinting.

Her laughter rippled out behind her as she sensed Piers at her back. She quickened her pace. When she felt a hand at her waist, she squealed. "No fair."

"What ever happened to warming up, stretching?"

"Didn't have the time."

"Take it." He paused, stopping her too. "Let's stretch."

For a couple of minutes they stretched, readying tight muscles for running.

"All set?"

"Yes."

Side by side they jogged into the desert behind Piers's home.

"I'll never understand how you found such a piece of property," Damiene said. "It's wonderful. Convenient to the city, yet right on the open desert too."

"Actually Vince found it for me when he first came out here. Found it in a week."

"What? That's very unusual, isn't it? Property must be expensive here."

"Vince is like a dog with a bone once he gets an idea in his head. When we both decided to relocate in America rather than stay in Europe, he wanted me to have a place near him that I would call home base."

She nodded, not answering because she needed to conserve her breath. And Piers wasn't even breathing hard. Miguel was wrong. Piers was in very good shape.

"Let's go down the arroyo," he said. "It's pretty there." Pointing past her to the declivity that seemed to form a path farther into the desert, Piers turned.

She followed him, panting now, but feeling comfortable, exhilarated. She always did when she was with Piers.

They hadn't gone more than another hundred yards when Piers's instincts started screaming out a warning. He looked around, instantly alert, but saw the flash of metal too late.

He felt the burning sensation in his shoulder and heard the crack of the rifle at almost the same moment. Fear for Damiene smothered him. Grabbing

her, he threw her to the ground behind some sa-
guaro cacti and dove down after her.

"Wha—what's wrong?" She tried to sit up, but he
pressed her into the ground.

"Someone's shooting," he said softly, peering back
over his shoulder.

"Oh, Piers" she moaned, twining her arms around
his neck. "You could have been killed, and it's because of me."

"Or me," he whispered, pushing her down even
flatter on the ground. "Stay there, love. I'm going to
try to get around to the back of him."

"No, don't go." Her whisper was low, frantic but
forceful. "There's blood on your sleeve. Piers, please."
She had to keep him safe. If she lost him, it would be
even more devastating than when Gilbert died. Far
worse than anything she could contemplate. Living
without Piers would be an agonizing waste of time.

He saw the fear in her eyes. "I'll be fine, darling.
Remember, I've lived on the edge a time or two. I can
be a very cautious guy."

"Piers, please. I can't lose you."

"You won't, not ever." He kissed her quickly, then
moved away from her, slithering on his belly.

In seconds he was out of sight and hearing.

Gritting her teeth, Damiene rolled over onto her
stomach and crept after him, trying to move as si-
lently as he. No way was she going to let him face
the man who wanted to shoot her . . . not on his
own.

Briars and low-growing cacti scratched her as she
inched after Piers. There were few clues to his trail
because he moved cleanly, not leaving many marks.
She figured several minutes had passed since the

shooting and she'd heard nothing nor caught any sign of Piers. Anxiety pulsed through her, and she had to fight the urge to get up and yell for him.

When an arm came out of nowhere and clamped around her mouth, fear exploded in her, blackness spinning behind her eyes. She was going to die.

"Be still. You little fool, you could get killed that way." Piers removed his hand from her mouth and put his lips there.

The kiss went on and on, deepening.

Damiene's relief turned to heat, and she clung to him. Then memory struck like a blow and she pulled back. "We have to hide." She mouthed the words at him.

He shook his head, wiping the damp tendrils of hair from her forehead. "Whoever it was left, and in a hurry. I saw where he was standing and the tire marks of his car."

She hugged him, her mind reeling with what could have happened. She might have lost Piers.

"Look at me." He put his hand under her chin. "I'm beginning to know you, love. And I'm reading in that mind of yours that you think it might be wise to leave me. It wouldn't be. No, don't interrupt. I thought at first it might be best for us to separate. I don't now—"

"But Piers—"

"I'm not letting you go, Damiene, and it isn't just that I want you near me, though that's certainly the main reason." He kissed her gently. "You're not thinking straight, love. That gunman could be after me."

"You can't believe that, not after the car incident and the trashing of my hotel room."

"I do believe it . . . and I think it's time you knew

more about my past so you'll accept it. Let's get a shower and a soak in the hot tub. We need to talk."

Damiene didn't move, her gaze fixed on the bloody sleeve of his sweatshirt. Nausea rose in her throat. "Your arm . . ."

"It's all right. He barely nicked me." He pulled her up with him and kept her hand in his as they headed back to the house.

Damiene couldn't believe there could be such danger in this beautiful sundrenched desert. Her fingers tightened around his.

Miguel met them at the door. "Bear called," he said succinctly. His gaze went to Piers's sleeve and he frowned. "What happened?"

"A scratch. Tell you later." He tapped Damiene on the nose. "You shower, darling, and I'll call Bear. Then we'll have our breakfast together."

"Your shoulder."

"I told you, it's nothing. I'll put some antiseptic and a small bandage on it."

"We should call the police." She shuddered at the thought of the questions they would ask.

"Not right away."

"All right." She said no more, watching as he trotted down the hall to his study. "Take care of him, Miguel."

Miguel nodded.

In his study Piers called Bear. His friend answered the phone immediately. "Bear? What's up?"

"Might be nothing. But the name Barnaby Echo has shown up again. In England.'

"What?"

"Yes, I felt the same way. I'm damned confused."

"How did you find out?"

"We didn't. Vince called me."

"I told him about Barnaby Echo."

"That's what he said. And then he told me that it was such an odd name, yet there'd been something familiar about it. He called his manager in his London club and ran the name by him. Sure enough, there was a connection. It seems there was a card game they used to play in the club many years ago, and its name was Barnaby Echo. A two-handed rummy-type game from the way he described it."

"Damn! That could be why it seemed strange but rang a bell. Another damned blind alley. I hate to tell Damiene. She counted on that name as a strong lead."

"Sorry. But at least we were able to run it down. We're filling in a few of the blanks."

"Yeah. We have to look at it that way." Still, Piers was disappointed. "Well, what else have we got?"

"Dolph hired somebody he knows in L.A., a private investigator who runs his own agency, used to be a homicide detective with the L.A. police until a disability sidetracked him. Dolph said he's good and has information lines to a great many places, including the FBI. He's got him nosing around about the car that almost hit you and Damiene."

"Good. What's his name?"

"Shim Locke."

"Great. Another unusual name. Have him get in touch with me when he can."

"Will do. Sorry about that Barnaby Echo thing. Going to tell Damiene?"

"Yes, and I'm going to tell her everything about Berto. It might keep her here with me. I know she has some cockamamy idea that what's been happening to us is somehow related to her alone."

"Something else?" Bear asked sharply.

"Yes. A sniper this morning. He disappeared."

"I'll call Dolph. He can relay that bit of news to Shim Locke."

"Fine. Talk to you later."

Piers hung up and strode from his study to his bedroom. He paused in the doorway when Damiene entered from the bathroom, a towel wrapped around her. "I'll shower and be with you in a second, love."

Damiene watched him disappear into the bathroom. It took all her willpower not to join him. She felt weepy and threatened. Not during her entire search for Barnaby Echo had she felt unsure of herself. There had been moments of trepidation, but she'd had a bulldog determination to carry through. Now, with the sniper hitting Piers, all that had changed. She wanted to crawl into a hole with Piers and tighten the lid.

Love was the great leveler, she thought. It sharpened focus and brought the important things to the forefront. She couldn't let Piers be in harm's way. No matter what it took, whatever dodge, she'd do it to insure his safety. Even if she had to leave.

Grief lanced her, crisscrossing her soul with razor-sharp cuts.

When Piers walked out of the bathroom, a towel around his waist and rubbing his head with another one, she embraced him and kissed him, trying to tell him with her body how very much she loved him.

"Wow! That I like." Piers hugged her tight.

"Breakfast?" she said weakly.

"For starters, yes."

They put on robes and headed for the kitchen. Miguel had left the oatmeal on the stove, and they served themselves large bowls of it. When they were seated side by side at the table, Piers faced her.

"I want to tell you about my past, my family, Berto, everything." He paused to collect his thoughts, eating absently. She waited patiently.

"My parents were both doctors," he began at last. "When I left for college, they sold their practice and joined a health organization that provided medical aid to third world countries in Africa. When I was at Oxford they both died of a fever that swept through the village where they had set up a clinic. They were buried there, as they had instructed in their wills."

Damiene felt the lonliness and sadness that must have been Piers's. "But you had an uncle."

"Yes, I had an uncle," he said, his voice bitter and ironical. "He died last year, as I told you. While he was alive he did his damnedest to keep control of the trust fund my parents had set up for me. I was twenty-two when they died, but my uncle was trustee of the fund until I was twenty-five." He smiled tightly. "I got the money from him before he spent it all, and there was bad blood between us from then on.

"The last time I saw him was about a year before he died, soon after Berto's death. He begged me to come see him in Sardinia and make up. He was staying there in the home of an Arab prince. There was a party the first night I was there, and the prince had set up several card games. I won a great deal of money, and the next thing I knew the prince was having me marched off by some armed guards, accusing me of cheating. I managed to get free and jumped through a glass door onto a terrace, then dove into the sea. It was a miracle I hit the water and not the rocks. I'm certain my uncle arranged all of it, telling the prince that I had insulted his honor by cheating and stealing his money from him."

"Oh, Piers," Damiene whispered. She pushed her bowl away and grasped his hand. "I understand how you must have felt. Truly I do."

"I wish I did," he said hoarsely, lifting her hand to his mouth to kiss it. "I haven't thought about my parents for a long time. I'd pushed them from my mind."

"They didn't choose to die and leave you," she said softly. "They had to help people, they were loving and giving. As for your uncle, he was pathetic and not worthy of hate."

"I know that . . . most of the time. But sometimes . . . it's hard to deal with."

She put her arms around him and kissed his cheek. "Your parents are still with you, Piers. Just forget your uncle. He can't touch you now."

"I know." He kissed her. "But thank you for saying it."

She studied his tight features. "And yet your parents, your uncle, and what happened to Berto are all mixed up in your mind."

He stiffened. "Maybe. I don't know. It's all so damned obscure." He exhaled heavily. "Berto was there for me when I was pretty down. He pushed and pulled at me, along with Dolph and Bear, to get my life on track. Berto and I bought our first casino in the Caribbean with money from my trust fund and some that we'd borrowed from Dolph and Bear. We paid them back within a year. Berto and I worked well together. We bought a second and a third casino, then got the big one in London. Things were booming for us. That night, the night he died, he told me to go home. I was taking an early morning flight the next day to the Caribbean. Two of the casinos down there had been losing money. Berto insisted that I go home and get some sleep. Five minutes later . . ." He shook his head. "The firemen couldn't even enter the place, it was so hot. I know I couldn't have helped him, but—"

"You feel guilty because you weren't there when it happened."

"Something like that."

"I understand that guilt feeling. I had it after Gilbert died, even when reason told me it wasn't my fault."

"You're right. And I know that too. But why Berto? Did the men who were skimming money from the casino kill him? I don't know, and I've *got* to know."

She squeezed his hand. "I understand that too."

He pulled her close. "It really helped to tell you about Berto. I needed to do that."

He lifted her from her chair and into his lap. "Until you came along, finding out who killed Berto and why was of prime importance in my life. Now you've pushed everything to the back of my mind. Once I'm sure you're safe, I'm going to tell my friends that the quest is over. I have no need to do anything more than take care of you."

"Sounds fine. I'll try to keep you occupied." When she felt his rumbling laugh, she experienced a rush of well-being that was new to her.

"I don't think you'll have too much trouble." He stared down at her when she pulled back from him, seeing the troubled expression in her eyes. "Unsure of what we have?"

"No. just wondering if I shouldn't give up my own fruitless search. I can't bring Gilbert back . . . and maybe the worry I'm giving my parents is simply causing them more grief."

"Do they know everything you're doing?"

She shook her head. "Some, but not all. They know I traced Barnaby Echo to Las Vegas."

"Damiene, love, I have to tell you something." He smoothed hair back from her forehead. "I found out that Barnaby Echo is a type of card game played in some of the private clubs in England." The disappointment in her face made him tighten his hold. "You did say you might want to give this up."

She nodded, pressing her face into his neck. "I guess now would be a good time." Then she pulled back again. "But what about the sniper and the car?"

Piers's smile tightened to a grim slash, sending shivers through her. "Yes. We need to do something about that."

Eight

"Don't be ridiculous, Piers," Bear said, watching his friend pace the length of Vince's office in the casino. "She's safe as a baby since you put that army of people around your place."

"I don't like being away from her. We're not any closer to finding the sniper than we were when it happened three days ago." Piers glared at his two relaxed friends.

"Vince told you," Bear said, "and I agree that the person might be relieved that you and your lady haven't been trying to stir up any more dirt. That sort of thing gets around, you know. You've been laying low these past few days, so maybe our shooter friend feels safe and is backing off."

"I know, Bear, that's logical."

"But you don't feel logical about the lady," Dolph said softly.

"No, I don't." Piers increased his pacing speed.

"And there's something else on your mind," Bear drawled.

Piers stopped. "It's not that important, I guess."

Come on, Piers," Dolph said. "You can tell us."

Piers hesitated, then muttered, "She damn well thinks I'm a gambler."

"So you are," Dolph said. "But are you saying she doesn't know that you're also a highly successful businessman?"

"She knows about the casinos, but not about the real estate," Piers murmured, shrugging. "Who'd ever guess that Berto and I would make so much money? We were a couple of reckless guys."

"Anyone who knew you then wouldn't be surprised," Bear said. "You and Berto together were like a super computer. That's probably why he left you his share of the business."

Piers nodded. "We figured we could protect our interests better if we were each other's beneficiary."

"At times you were a wild man after Berto died," Dolph mused. "When you bet on that car race across the desert, then drove it yourself, I was sure you would've come a cropper on that one. But you won again."

"I'd had a tip that the person who'd torched the club was a mechanic in the race." Piers shook his head. "Never found the mechanic, but the race paid off in other ways."

"I should have driven," Bear said sourly. "You could have cracked up out there."

"You bet on me," Piers reminded him, his mood lightening.

"And since then you've played cards and rolled dice and made more money."

"Right. Gambling is a damned good cover whenever I want to follow a lead. That race was one of those leads." He frowned. "Rustam Dever surfaced as a high winner in that race."

Dolph studied his friend. "You still think he was in on it, don't you?"

"I know he was, but I can't get a thing on him."

Bear shook his head. "I can't believe Dever would be dumb enough to go after Berto. He knows you'd think of him right away."

Piers nodded. "I still think he was in on it. And someday I'll prove it."

"Does Damiene know about Dever and how you feel about him?" Dolph asked.

"She has a pretty good idea." He sighed. "But Damiene doesn't know I'm . . . I've . . ."

"That you're the head of a highly successful corporation?" Bear asked.

"Yeah." Piers started pacing again. "None of us figured it would happen to me either."

"You were always pretty careless with money," Dolph said. "When you started buying up those run-down places in the Caribbean, even Berto laughed at you."

Piers smiled. "But he still went in on it with me. He thought I was a damned fool, but he backed me anyway."

"Too bad he isn't around to enjoy the fruits of what he called your hare-brained schemes."

"Yes." Bear looked around him. "Vince has done a good job for himself with this place. He should expand his holdings too."

Piers shrugged. "I've told him that, but he says he isn't ready."

"Berto used to hang over his shoulder when he worked in the club in London, but I think he'd be proud of Vince and this place."

"Getting back to Damiene, Piers," Dolph said somberly. "I think you should tell her about your business. Women don't mind a rich man."

His cynical tone turned Piers toward him. "Dolph, don't judge all women by the actions of some."

"I try not to," Dolph said colorlessly.

"Just tell her that you can take care of her," Bear suggested, "that she won't have to worry about keeping the wolf from the door."

"Damiene is a CPA," Piers said dryly, "and has her own accounting firm."

Bear shrugged. "I always avoid the intelligent ones."

"Oh?" Dolph said. "Which one of us was in love with the college professor?"

"Dolph, my friend, I told you I broke that off as soon as she asked me to write a precis of my actions from birth."

"I'd like to have read that." Dolph smiled. "You'd have to fill in the details of that fight in Nice. I'm still not clear on that."

"It was nothing. Put it out of your mind."

"Bear, my friend, I'm the one who spent the night in jail. I'd like to know the details.'

"Ah, so you were." Bear grinned but said no more.

"I hate to break up this intriguing conversation," Piers said, "but I need to get back to Damiene. See you later."

He strode from the room, closing the door sharply behind him. Bear and Dolph stared at each other, smiling slowly.

• • •

Damiene wandered around the house, feeling restless, fidgety. Finally she went into Piers's study and called her parents.

"Mom? Yes, it's Damiene. I'm going to be coming home. I don't think I can go any further on this search. Maybe now we should put Gilbert to rest. I know you want me home." She paused. "Mother, I've met a wonderful man. Yes, he makes me happy. Yes, I'd like to bring him home. I'll talk to him. Give my love to Daddy. I love you, Mom." When she cradled the receiver, she swiped at her eyes. Her mother needed some peace. Putting an end to this quest for Gilbert's killers might give her a measure of that.

Going out into the hall, she stopped short, seeing Miguel. "Hello, I almost ran into you."

Miguel nodded. "I thought you might like a cool drink," he said, handing her a glass. It's getting hot."

"Sounds wonderful. Maybe I'll go for a swim too." She took a long swallow from the glass and sighed. "That's good. A combination of juices, isn't it?"

"Sí. Papaya, orange, and pineapple. It was mixed for us specially."

"Umm. Thank you. I think I'll swim now."

Miguel nodded and returned to the kitchen, and Damiene went on to the solarium. She finished the juice, then changed into her suit. Her cap and goggles on, she strode to the pool and dove in. Pain suddenly pierced her head, and she blamed it on the cool water after being so warm.

She was on her second lap when she felt a searing cramp. Stunned, she swallowed water. Instinct had her heading for the side of the pool, but she was overcome by dizziness and nausea.

Blackness smothered her, and she didn't even try to fight the rush of water into her nose and mouth as she sank.

Piers walked into the house, noting the stillness right away. Too quiet. "Damiene! Miguel!"

Running to the master suite took only seconds. He sprinted out of there, calling to Miguel. Nothing! Where the hell were they?

He passed the kitchen and tore into the solarium, spotting her in the pool at once. His body knifed through the air and into the water. In seconds he had her in his arms, turning her, breathing into her mouth. "Dammit, Damiene, breathe," he muttered when he was able to lift her to the side. Again and again he breathed into her.

When she coughed, he praised God.

"That's it, Damiene. Breathe, breathe."

Damiene retched, coughing up pool water, losing the contents of her stomach on the pool surround.

"Easy, darling." Piers wrapped her in a towel he took from the stand near the pool. "Shh, easy, relax. I have you."

She opened her eyes. "Piers. What happened?"

"I don't know. I found you facedown in the water."

"Cramp. Then I got dizzy and sick." She closed her eyes.

"Lie still. I'm going to get an ambulance."

She didn't open her eyes, nor answer.

Not looking away from her, Piers dialed emergency. "Yes, yes, she's conscious now, but she was unconscious when I pulled her from the pool. Hurry."

Returning to her, he scooped her into his arms,

alarmed that she was so limp. Seeing that she was breathing more easily, he eased her back onto the floor, then strode over to the intercom. "Miguel? Miguel, where are you? Dammit, man, speak to me."

In minutes the ambulance roared up the drive with another car right behind it. Piers led the paramedics to the solarium, then jumped when a hand fell on his shoulder.

"Relax, Piers. it's Dolph."

He glanced away from Damiene for a moment to look at his friend. "How did you know?"

"Vince had his police radio on and we heard the call. Are you all right?'

"Yes. Damiene . . . she said she had a cramp, but I think somehow someone got to her."

"Don't worry, Piers, we'll—"

Dolph was interrupted by an angry exclamation from Bear, and he and Piers looked up to see Bear and Vince striding toward them.

"What's going on?" Piers asked.

Bear gestured to the kitchen. "Vince just found Miguel on the floor in the kitchen. He looks bad."

Piers cursed viciously. "Tell the paramedics. We'll take him with Damiene. Who was here? What the hell is going on?"

"Easy, man," Dolph said as Piers flexed his hands into fists. "You go to the hospital with those two. The three of us will stay here and look around. Get going."

Vince sat slumped in a chair by the pool, tipping a beer into his mouth. "I don't get it."

"Then let's take it apart," Dolph said. "We've been

all over the house. No sign of forced entry, or of a struggle of any kind."

Bear smacked his hand on the table in front of him. "From what Piers said, she was out cold in the water, that she wouldn't have lasted much longer."

Dolph's mouth tightened. "And what happened to Miguel?"

Vince shrugged. "Hit on the head, drugs? who knows?"

"Did he have a wound on him?"

"Not that I could see, but the medics didn't think he was in good shape."

Piers stayed with Damiene as they pumped her stomach, overriding every argument of the medics and nurses.

"You're not her husband, sir, and—"

"I soon will be and I'm staying."

It seemed to take forever before Damiene was pronounced in good shape. As they moved her to a room, the doctor told Piers she would sleep for several hours. Depending on what they discovered when they analyzed the contents of her stomach, she could probably go home the next day.

Relieved, Piers asked about Miguel.

The doctor shook his head. "I'm sorry, but he's in serious condition. Does he have family?"

"He has no one but me. May I see him?"

"All right, but I'm not sure he'll know you."

In the private hospital room, Piers looked down at the man who'd been at his side for five years. Miguel was frighteningly still and pale.

"He's hanging on," the doctor said, "but it's touch and go."

"What happened to him?"

"I suspect that both he and Miss Belson were poisoned. But we also found a stab wound in your friend's back which has caused internal bleeding. That's what's taken the toll. He's in very good physical shape and that's going to help him."

"Do everything possible. Please." Piers reached down and touched one flaccid hand. "Miguel. Amigo."

As though the whispered words penetrated the almost lifeless body, Miguel's eyelids fluttered and opened.

"Shh, Miguelito, don't talk." Piers tried to quiet him, but there was obviously something Miguel had to say.

Grasping Piers's wrist, he strained himself. "No . . . amigo . . ." Miguel gasped, then fell back.

"Miguel," Piers said, but he didn't need the doctor's shake of his head to tell him that his friend had passed out.

"I'm sorry, Mr. Larraby." The doctor signaled that they leave the room. "He has a chance."

"Thank you."

As the doctor walked away, Piers puzzled over Miguel's words. It was clear he'd needed to say them, and had used a good share of his strength to do it. But why would he say he was not his friend?

Going back to Damiene's room, he put it from his mind. As he entered the room, he breathed a sigh of relief. Her color was better. He sat down beside the bed and took her limp hand in both of his. Staring at her, he tried not to think what would have happened if he'd found her even a minute later.

He was still sitting there half an hour later when the door opened behind him. He leapt out of the chair and whirled around, his hands in the ready position of karate.

"Take it easy," Dolph said. "Its' just me."

Piers dropped his hands. "I'm not taking any more chances, Dolph. I'll kill anyone, without a qualm, who comes near her if I think they're threatening her."

"We're going to take care of her too," Dolph said gently. "She'll be fine."

"I can't let anything happen to her."

"You'd die without her. I can see that. I swear to you, she'll be fine."

Piers shot a quick look at Damiene, then gazed at his friend. "Did you know that Miguel has a stiletto-type wound in his back?"

Dolph shook his head. "They're getting bolder."

"Yes. Strange, isn't it? Damiene and I had just decided to give up on our quests."

"Are you saying you're through looking for Berto's killer?"

"Yes, I am. I want a life with Damiene, and vengeance doesn't make a good companion to happiness."

"But whoever it is you're chasing obviously doesn't know this," Dolph said softly.

"No." Piers smacked one hand into the palm of the other.

"I've arranged for guards for both Damiene and Miguel."

Piers nodded.

"But you'll be staying with her."

"Yes. I'm going to marry her as soon as she'll let me," Piers said hoarsely.

Dolph allowed himself a small smile. "That's not news. Piers, you're a lucky man."

"I know." His expression hardened. "If only I knew who the hell the enemy was so I could deal with him, or kill him."

"We might do that for you."

Piers's gaze sharpened on him. "You know something?"

"No, but we will. Bear and I are moving into Vince's place. We're on this full-time, the three of us, until it's over."

Piers relaxed slightly. "Thanks."

"I can remember the night in London when you took a bullet for me, mate." Dolph slipped into the Aussie accent he sometimes adopted. He never mentioned those years on the island continent, even to his best friends.

Piers shook his head. "Anybody who didn't know you would swear you'd been born down under. How is it you can master accents and speech patterns so easily?"

"Part of an actor's makeup, chum." Dolph's deprecating smile didn't hide all the bitterness in his face.

"You were not responsible, Dolph," Piers said softly.

Dolph looked away. "Most days I believe that."

"Bear was there that night, too, friend. His jaw was moved over a couple of inches, as I recall."

"I appreciate that neither of you pushed me to explain everything about that night," Dolph said colorlessly.

"You said it was not your secret to reveal," Piers reminded him.

"So I did." Dolph looked sour for a moment, then

he smiled. "And I'd thought until then that only a freight train could've damaged Bear's jaw."

"The two men who did it looked like an engine and caboose."

Damiene heard voices, but the people had to be far away. Down a long tunnel with fuzzy light at the end. She had to get there. Trying to run was difficult. Nothing moved. Were her legs tied? The voices were getting louder. Did she know one? "Piers? Piers!" Her shout was almost soundless, croaky.

"Open your eyes, darling. I'm here."

"Are you? Hold me. Don't let me go." Had she been drinking? Her mind was hazy.

"I'll never let you go. Marry me right away."

"All right." She yawned and went back to sleep.

"Damn," Piers said softly, pulling the blanket up to her chin. "I don't believe you did that."

Dolph burst out laughing. "I heard that little exchange. You'll never live that down."

Bear came into the room. "He won't live what down?"

"He asked Damiene to marry him right away and she fell asleep."

"She said yes first," Piers insisted, his smile widening when his friends laughed. "Get out of here, peons."

"Come on, Dolph," Bear said. "Vince has already gone back to his place. Since we'll be moving in with him, he wanted to clean out a space for us." He grinned at Dolph. "You get to sleep in a dresser drawer."

"Amusing."

Bear turned to Piers. "What should we do?"

Piers breathed in shakily. "Notify the police. The doctor thinks both of them may have been poisoned. See if there's any food around that they both might have eaten." He stared hard at his two friends. "We're going to find who did this."

That night when Piers finally dropped off in a cot too short and narrow for his frame, the constant rattle of hospital noises barely penetrated his deep sleep. But when Damiene groaned, he was on his feet in a flash, looking first at the bed, then around the room. No one.

He leaned over the bed. "What is it, darling? Easy. Don't thrash like that. I'm here."

Her eyes snapped open, looking straight at him. "Danger. I felt it."

He smiled at her. "It's all right. I'm staying right in the room with you and there's a guard outside. No one will hurt you."

"Hold me, Piers," she murmured, and fell asleep with his arms around her.

He could have pulled free of her, but instead, he inched her over and climbed in beside her. If anything, it was more uncomfortable than the steel cot, but it comforted him to be with her, and he was soon asleep.

The next morning the nurse woke him, smothering a smile. "This is hardly hospital procedure, Mr. Larraby."

"Oh?" Piers yawned behind his hand, wincing at the muscle aches from sleeping so cramped up. He rubbed his bristly chin and looked down at Damiene. She was awake and looking from him to the nurse, a flush of embarassment creeping over her face. He laughed and kissed her.

On the drive home from the hospital later that morning, Damiene kept shooting looks at Piers.

"All right," he said, "what is it? Something's bothering you."

"That nurse didn't know whether to laugh or call security when she came into my room this morning."

"Nurses are tough," he drawled.

"You didn't have to tell her that I insisted you sleep with me."

"Technically it's true. You were much more comfortable after I got into bed with you."

She rested her head back on the seat and chuckled. "I'm weak as a kitten, but I feel good." The silence from Piers pulled her gaze to him. "What is it?"

"The doctor told me what he's already told you— that you had enough of a curare-type poison in your system to render you helpless."

"Yes, I know that." She drew in a shaky breath. "What do I recall about what happened? Is that the next question?"

"Yes."

"Don't grit your teeth that way. You'll take the enamel off."

"Damiene!"

"I remember drinking some fruit juice—"

"The police found that and what was in it matched up with what was in your system and Miguel's."

"By the way, how is he?"

Piers reached out a hand and squeezed her thigh. "We'll talk when we get home."

"Piers . . . tell me. Will he be all right?" Piers nodded. "But he's bad, isn't he? I can't believe it. Did he ingest more of the poison than I?" Shaken, she looked at Piers when he didn't answer right away. "Piers?"

"There was a stab wound in his back. That's why his condition is so serious. Internal bleeding."

"Lord! What's going on, Piers?"

"I don't know, but I will." He pulled in the long, curving drive to the house, then stopped in front of it. "Damiene. I promised you I'd give up the search for Berto's killers, and I fully meant to honor that promise. Now things have changed."

Fear flashed in her eyes.

He gripped her shoulders. "Don't look like that. It's not that I want—"

"Whoever poisoned Miguel and me could be after you."

"Or you."

"No, that doesn't make sense. Piers, it's too dangerous. Let's get away. Go to Hawaii. Anywhere."

"Sounds wonderful . . . but I can't, sweetheart. I can't let anyone threaten you."

She covered his hands with hers. "Then let's run, hide. Can't we let someone else look for the killer?"

He released her and got out of the car. She watched him as he walked around the car and opened her door.

"You're not going to run, are you? " she asked. "You're going to hunt down the people you've been searching for and face them. Aren't you?"

He helped her from the car. "Careful. You're still a little rocky. I've arranged for the sister of one of Vince's dealers to come out and be a temporary housekeeper."

"You didn't answer my question."

"Damiene, you must see that we have to get to the bottom of this. The danger isn't just going to melt away. Let's go inside. We need to talk."

Damiene had a shivery, uncomfortable feeling that she wasn't going to like what Piers had to say.

She paused in the spacious tiled foyer of the adobe house, feeling at home . . . but like an alien too. She expected any moment to see the taciturn Miguel approach her.

"Feeling strange?" Piers put his hand on the small of her back, guiding her toward the master suite.

"Yes." she faced him in the bedroom, lifting her chin. "What did you want to say?"

"Loaded for bear, are you?"

"I feel I'd better be."

"All right. I'll cut to the chase. Damiene, I feel that you should return to your parents' home and—"

"Oh, no, that I won't do." He was going to do something to draw out the enemy, endanger himself!

"Yes, you will, if I have to truss you like a turkey and put you on the plane myself."

"I'm not leaving. So you can put a sock in it, buster."

Nine

Piers tossed and turned. He was in his own bed. There was a cool breeze coming off the desert. All was conducive to sleep, but he couldn't. He wanted to hold Damiene, love her. But he feared her power that night. There was no way he would let her stay in Las Vegas when he, Bear, and Dolph decided to pull out the stops.

They'd even excluded Vince from their plans. It made Piers ill to think of something happening to Berto's only brother. No way was Vince going to be involved if things got heavy. And, though he didn't know why, Piers felt as though they were getting close, that the answer was almost in his grasp. Something had panicked the enemy into nasty action, and Piers knew he'd show his hand soon.

Damiene slept fitfully. It hadn't helped her rest to realize that Piers wasn't going to be joining her.

She'd wrestled with the notion of going to his bed, but she hadn't. He was angry with her and adamant. Well, she could be determined too. Piers Larraby would find that out.

When she finally rose she felt dry-eyed and strained. She changed into a swim suit and left the room. Padding down the hall to the main section of the house, she paused when she heard rustling in the kitchen.

Entering the room, she saw a woman washing vegetables in the sink. "Hello, I'm Damiene Belson."

The woman whirled around, smiling. "You startled me, miss. I'm Lona, the housekeeper."

"How do you do. Do you know where Mr. Larraby is?"

"Yes, he went into Las Vegas early this morning. He said he was meeting with his friends and that he'd be back by noon."

Damiene nodded. "All right. I'm going to take a swim now." She knew she had to rid herself of the insistent fears that had attacked her since she'd woken up in the hospital. Facing the pool was the only way to do that.

"Oh, do you want me to watch you, miss?" Lona asked. "I know it isn't safe to swim alone." The woman's face was creased in concern.

"You're right," Damiene said, unable to repress the shudder that shook her. "Perhaps if you just looked out there now and then."

"I'm amazed that you would want to swim after . . ." Lona's voice trailed off, her face reddening. "Mr. Dalrymple told me about your accident."

"I see. Well, maybe if you did keep watch it would

be better, thank you. I hope it won't be too much trouble."

"None at all, miss." Relief flashed across the woman's face.

Damiene stood at the side of the pool for a long moment, staring down into the water. She couldn't work up the nerve to dive in, so she sat on the edge and let herself slip in. After a moment she sank down, submerging her whole self. Panic fluttered inside her, but she battled it and it began to subside. Relieved, she pushed away from the side and began to swim, her arms and legs moving rhythmically, her speed and power increasing along with her confidence.

She had only done five laps when she saw Lona waving to her, the phone held in her hand.

Stopping, Damiene took deep breaths and nodded, then she vaulted up to the pool surround. She snatched a towel from the table and dried her face as she strode to the housekeeper.

"Hello," she said into the phone. "Yes, this is Damiene Belson. Just a moment, please." She pulled the cap off her head and placed the receiver tight to her ear. "What were you saying?"

"My name is Dr. Westmore, Miss Belson, at General Hospital in Rochester. Are you related to John and Ethel Benson?"

Her grip tightened on the phone. "Yes, they're my parents. What's happened?"

"I'm sorry, Miss Belson, but they were in a car accident. I'm afraid both of them were badly injured. They're in surgery now. We found your name and this phone number in your mother's purse."

"Oh my God." She drew in a shuddering breath, fear choking her. "Dr. Westmore . . . will they . . . what are their chances?"

"It's hard to say. We have a very good staff here—"

"Please, please help them. I'm coming right away. I'll catch the first plane out."

Lona approached Damiene as she hung up the phone. "I couldn't help overhearing. Is there anything I can do?"

"Yes. Could you call the airlines and book me on a flight, any flight, final destination Rochester, New York?" Damiene was shaking. "My parents were in an accident. The doctor didn't sound too hopeful." She bit her lip. "I have to go."

"Of course, miss, I'll call at once."

"Thank you." She gasped back a sob. "I'll have to leave a note for Piers. . . ."

"I'll tell him what happened, miss. You go pack and I'll get you a flight."

In short order, Damiene had packed a carry-on bag with the bare necessities, and had changed into a turquoise polished cotton jumpsuit. She left a note on Piers's dressing table, then met Lona at the front door.

"I could have called you a cab, miss—"

"That's all right. I'll take Mr. Larraby's Cherokee and leave it at the airport with the keys under the accelerator."

"I'll tell him, miss."

In minutes Damiene was on the road, surprised by the heavy traffic at such an early hour. Fear and confusion gripped her as she thought of what had happened to her parents. They were careful drivers.

But then, she remembered Gilbert's friends had died in a car crash, a crash that she was certain had been no accident. Tightly grasping the wheel, she forced from her mind the horrible thought that someone might have tried to kill her parents.

She arrived at the airport only fifteen minutes before her flight was due to leave. After parking and putting the keys under the accelerator, she shouldered her bag and started for the terminal.

The honking of a horn made her turn, and she was relieved to see an airport shuttle pull up.

The driver opened the doors. "Airport shuttle, miss. Need a ride to the terminal?"

"Oh, please. Thanks." She stepped up into the empty minibus and moved past the driver toward the seats.

The blow caught her behind the ear and she collapsed without a sound.

Piers strode toward the house, frowning at the open garage where the Cherokee was kept. Had Damiene taken it out? Dammit, she should have waited for him. Wasn't it bad enough he'd had a sleepless night because of her? Did he need to be worrying about her careering over the countryside in the four-wheeler? Damn her! He wasn't going to back down on this. She was going back to her parents on the first flight.

"Lona!"

The woman came pattering from the back of the house into the foyer. "Yes, Mr. Larraby?"

"Is Miss Belson out in the Cherokee?"

"Yes, she is. She—"

"Why the hell didn't you stop her?" Piers put up a hand when the woman looked stunned. "Sorry. I'm not trying to bully you. I just don't want her driving around by herself, yet."

"Sir, I'm trying to tell you. Miss Belson is gone, Mr. Larraby. She's flying home." Lona fumbled in her pocket, pulling a crumpled piece of paper from it. "Here it is. Flight number and everything into O'Hare. Miss Belson was going to try to buy a ticket from there to Rochester, New York."

Open-mouthed, Piers took the piece of paper. Damiene hadn't said good-bye. "I see."

"I don't think so, sir. You see, she got a call when she was in the pool—"

"In the pool? Alone? Damn, why doesn't she listen to me?"

"Sir, I was watching her. It seems her parents had an accident."

"What?" Piers focused on the housekeeper. "Tell me."

"There's a note in your bedroom for you, but Miss Belson's parents were in an auto accident. A doctor called her here."

Piers ran down the hall, Lona's words ringing in his ears.

In the bedroom he ripped open the envelope and read the three paragraphs twice.

"Damn," he muttered, then strode to the phone and dialed quickly. "Dolph? Is Bear with you? Good, put me on the speaker phone. Listen to this." He read the note. "I don't like it."

"It sounds pretty straightforward to me," Bear says.

"She's got the doctor's name, the name of the hospital. Wouldn't she ask all the right questions before she left?"

"Maybe, but she could also be so upset by such news that she'd react quickly and not logically."

"All right, we'll get on it. What are you going to do?"

"I'm going to the airport. I'll verify the flight she's booked on and go from there. I may be leaving the city."

"Going after her?"

"Yes." He hung up and hurried down the hall to the kitchen. "Lona, I'm going to the airport. I'll let you know if I'll be leaving the area."

"All right." As soon as she saw his car tear down the driveway, she lifted the phone and dialed a number. "Yes," she said to the man on the other end. "He just left for the airport. I hope you'll be able to help them. Well, thank you, I try." Lona replaced the receiver and returned to the kitchen, humming while she worked. She'd helped Mr. Larraby, and that made her feel good. He as a fine man.

Piers broke a few speed laws getting to the airport, but he had no intention of stopping even if he were flagged by a cop. Damiene needed him! Of that he was very sure.

If anything happened to her . . . But he couldn't go on thinking that way. It would cloud his reasoning and his reactions.

Tires screeching, he slammed on the brakes in front of the airport terminal. Leaving the car in a towaway zone, he raced inside. Scanning the monitor, he saw her flight had left thirty minutes before. He almost hoped she was on it.

She wasn't.

"No, sir," the ticket agent told him. "Miss Belson did not pick up her ticket."

"Thanks," Piers said grimly. He went right to a public phone and called Bear and Dolph.

"Your suspicions were correct," Dolph said. "We called the hospital in Rochester. No record of a Mr. or Mrs. Belson being admitted today. No record of a Dr. Westmore either."

"Dammit, where the hell is she?"

"We'll find her," Bear said gruffly.

"Yeah. Dolph, get your PI friend Locke in on this. We need to find her fast."

"Will do."

Piers hung up the phone and leaned his forehead against the cool plastic. Think! Think!

The car! He sprinted out of the terminal. Thank God, the Cherokee was red. In minutes he'd spotted it and was running across the parking lot.

The car was empty, the keys under the accelerator. Looking around, he saw nothing that would help him except . . . he stared down at the footprints trailing from a small puddle of oil. She'd been in a hurry, so she wouldn't have seen it.

The footprints ended abruptly. He frowned down at them, combing his fingers restlessly through his hair. He didn't notice when a shuttle bus pulled up alongside him.

"Need a ride to the terminal, sir?" the driver asked, opening the doors.

"No, I—" Piers looked sharply at the man. "Wait a minute." He pulled a photo of Damiene from his pocket. "Did you happen to pick this woman up about an hour ago?"

The driver looked at the picture and shook his head. "Sorry, sir. I don't recognize her. But we've got four different shuttle buses. I could ask the other drivers."

Piers nodded. "I'd appreciate it." He took out his card and scribbled Vince's office number on it. "Have someone call me at either of these places."

"Sure thing. She's a pretty woman, sir. I hope you find her."

"So do I," Piers muttered.

He returned to the terminal and called information in Rochester, New York, asking for Damiene's parents.

"Hello. Mr. Belson? I'm Piers Larraby, a friend of your daughter's. Oh, she did mention me. Good. Sir, have either you or your wife been in an accident? I know it's a strange question. No sir, there's no reason for you to come out here. I can handle everything. I don't think she's in danger, sir, but she might be on a wild goose chase. Of course, I'll be glad to call you. Thank you."

Piers had no compunction about glossing over the truth to Damiene's father. From what she'd told him, they'd had enough emotional stress to last a lifetime. He wouldn't put any more on their plate . . . unless it became necessary.

Dialing again, he drummed on the phone with his fingers until it was answered. "Bear, I can't find her. Not a clue. I'm coming back to Vince's. I have a bad feeling about this. I'll be there soon."

All during the drive to Vince's Piers went over every bit of information he had. He knew the tiniest thing could be important. Don't concentrate on the big picture, he told himself. Keep the details in the front of the brain.

Speeding along the highway, he wove dangerously among the other cars. In a detached way he tried to imagine what Bear would say about his driving. His good friend was as cold as ice on the track, and ruthless. Off the track, though, he was the safest driver Piers had ever seen. Bear would probably break both his arms if he saw the way he tore through the city, turning the wrong way on a one-way street to get to the back entrance of Vince's casino.

He squealed to a halt outside the door and leapt from the car. The door was locked. Cursing, he kicked it with all his might until an employee opened it.

"Thanks," he muttered, hurrying past the man and down the long corridor to Vince's office.

Throwing open the door, he stared at Bear. "Where are Vince and Dolph?"

"Vince is out with some of his people scouring the countryside for Damiene. Dolph got a call from Shim Locke. He should be back anytime."

"I need to talk to Vince." He had picked up the receiver and was dialing the number of Vince's car phone when the door opened behind him. He turned to see Dolph usher two other men into the room.

"Hello, Piers," Dolph said casually. "I don't believe you've met Shim Locke." He indicated a slim, dark-haired man. "But I know you've met Rustam Dever."

He shoved Dever into the room, and Piers saw that Locke had a gun, which he kept trained on Dever.

"I'll see you and your friends in jail, Larraby," Dever snarled at him.

Piers grabbed the man, his hand closing around his throat. "What have you been up to? Did you take Damiene?"

"Go to hell." Dever struggled to free himself, and Piers tightened his hand around his throat. Rustam's bluster faded. His face turned red, no sound came from his open mouth, his eyes were wild.

"Don't throttle him, Piers," Bear said mildly. "He'll talk, won't you, Rustam? We won't let him kill you if you tell us where Damiene is. As it is, you'll go to prison for a long time, but at least you'll be alive. Kidnapping is a federal offense."

Piers released him, and Dever backed away. He stared at them, rubbing his throat, hatred and fear warring in his eyes. "All right, all right, I'll tell you, but I want a deal—"

"No deals," Piers grated. "Where is she?"

"I didn't wanna kill her—"

Piers leapt at him. It took all of Dolph's strength to hold him.

Bear grabbed Dever. "Where is she?"

"I don't know. He took her." He glanced fearfully at Piers. "Don't let him near me."

"I'll let him tear you apart unless you tell us who's got her and where she is," Bear said tightly.

"Barnaby Echo," Dever said hoarsely.

"Damn you, that's a game," Bear said, gripping the front of his shirt.

"I know, but it's his trade name, too, the name he uses in the business." Dever shrank back when Piers tried to go for him again. "It's the truth."

"Who's Barnaby Echo?" Bear asked.

"I think I know," Piers said. "Damn his soul. It's Vince, isn't it?"

Dever nodded. "He's used the name for years. Got it from a game he used to play with his brother. Vince said Berto used to call him that when they were kids." Dever's gaze shifted nervously from one man to the other. "I didn't want any of this. It was his idea to kill Berto . . . and you. Not mine."

Dolph stiffened. "Why would he want to kill Piers?"

"He was getting too close. And when this Belson lady started nosing around and he teamed up with her— Hey!"

Piers shook him. "Where is she?"

"I told you, I don't know!"

"Then tell me why. Why her? Why her brother?"

"Tell him," Bear said softly, "or so help me, I'll cripple you by inches."

"We didn't think she'd ever come out here," Dever blurted. "As for her brother, he turned squeamish when he found out his friends were in Atlantic City to pick up ten kilos of heroin to take back to Rochester. He freaked out." Dever shrugged. "Even though he didn't know our names, he'd heard Vince's cover name. He had to go. But I didn't kill him."

"Heroin?" Dolph asked.

"Vince has been laundering money for the mob for years. Sometimes he acts as a middleman for them." Dever was sweating profusely now. "Vince borrowed some money from your places, Larraby. His brother caught him. I guess Berto thought he could straighten out Vince." Dever shook his head. "Vince would kill anybody who got in his way."

Piers shook him again. "Where is Vince now?"

"I swear to God, I don't know."

Dolph gestured to Shim Locke. "Keep him under

cover until we find Miss Belson. If you hear anything, call me here or in the car."

"Yes, sir."

When they left, Piers hit the desktop with his fist.
"Damn! It was Vince all along. He was the one who
found Miguel. That must have been what Miguel
was trying to tell me in the hospital. He must have
been semiconscious when Vince stabbed him. Somehow he knew."

Dolph began pacing. "He's always been there, whenever anything happened. He knew our every move."

"That car the night I met Damiene," Piers said
tightly. "Was it because he recognized her, or was it
a setup for me? He connects up with her brother
because of—"

"Barnaby Echo," Bear finished softly. "Damn, where
were our eyes? He was in on everything we did. Why
didn't we go into that Barnaby Echo thing in depth?
We accepted his glib explanation without a second
thought."

"He's a friend," Dolph said. "Or so we thought.
And he's smart. He knows how intensely we've been
on this. You're in danger, Piers."

"Aren't we all," he whispered. "It's Damiene who
concerns me. I need to find her."

"You'll find her. We'll find her," Bear said huskily.

"He must be near the city. He wouldn't risk a long
trip." Dolph shook his head. "But where?"

"Think," Bear said. "Where would he take her?
Dolph's right. It won't be too far from here. He'll
want to . . ." His voice trailed off and his glance
shifted away from Piers.

"You think he'll kill her as quickly as possible,"
Piers said woodenly.

"It makes sense," Bear answered.

"Wait a minute," Dolph said, stopping his pacing. "He probably wouldn't take her to a building. He wants to dispose of her. Sorry, Piers."

"Go on," Piers said sharply.

"To dispose of her in a house could leave traces. Vince has both a van and a truck. In the early days of the casino, he used to lug his own trash out to that abandoned dump off the mountain highway."

"I've heard him mention it more than once," Bear said slowly.

"I need a chopper."

"Piers, you haven't flown in some time."

"I can still handle a helicopter, Dolph." He picked up the phone. "What's the number of that airfield on the outskirts of town?"

"I'll get it for you," Dolph said, taking the phone from him.

"We'll be on your tail with the police," Bear said as Dolph called the airfield.

"I know that."

Dolph hung up the phone. "It's yours. He'll have it gassed and warmed up for you. Take care, pal."

"Right." Piers sprinted out the door as Dolph called the police.

Damiene's mouth was dry and her head hurt badly. If only she could swallow. She had something tied around her mouth and eyes, and her hands and feet were bound. What happened? She remembered going to the airport. Her parents!

She struggled to sit up, and heard movement behind her. The gag was pulled roughly from her mouth.

She licked her lips and swallowed. "Who are you? And why am I here? I have a plane to catch—"

"To see your parents in the hospital," a man said. "That worked well."

She stiffened. She knew that voice, that distinctive British accent. "Vince!"

He laughed. "You never suspected, did you?"

He pulled her blindfold off, and she looked around desperately. She seemed to be in the back of a van. Vince was squatting beside her.

"Where's Piers?" she asked hoarsely.

"I'm hoping he'll be joining you soon."

The glitter in his eyes was frightening. "Could you untie me?"

"I think not."

There was an unhealthy urgency about him, a musky smell of sweat and fear. Sensing growing peril, Damiene told herself to keep him talking. "Did you leave the juice at the house?"

"Did you enjoy it? You should have died then. It would have been painless."

"And you were driving the car that almost hit me, weren't you?"

"Ah, yes, the happy night you met my friend, Piers. No, someone else was doing the driving, not me. Pity he missed. I could've gotten both of you. All this mess would be behind me now."

"Is Piers coming here?"

"No, I intend to collect him after you're attended to, Miss Damiene Belson."

"Did you know my brother?" she blurted out, throwing caution to the winds.

"In a way. He foolishly involved himself in a very high-priced drug deal. His pals were making a little money on the side transporting heroin from Atlantic City to Rochester. But your brother objected. And since he'd heard my cover name . . ." He shrugged with a chilling nonchalance.

"Barnaby Echo," she whispered.

"Yes, that was a pet name my brother had for me . . . and it was a card game, incidentally, but only in my family." Vince shook his head. "You've really been a thorn in my side, Damiene. You and your brother." His look suddenly became vicious. "And I took care of my own damned brother when he found out I had 'borrowed' some funds from the casinos he and Piers owned."

"Piers has nothing to do with this."

"Oh, but he does. He has the casinos I want. My damned brother made Piers his principal heir, so I got peanuts. I'm doing well, but I want it all. It's rightfully mine. Besides, Piers is in love with you. If you disappear, he'll turn the world upside down and sideways looking for you." Vince gnashed his teeth. "I don't want him on my tail."

"No! He has other interests."

"Miss Belson, don't try to con a con man. It won't work." He opened the door of the van. "Let's go."

"I can't go anywhere with my feet tied." At that moment Damiene made the decision to die fighting. Why make it easy for a bastard like Vince? He'd killed her brother and he would try to kill Piers. She would do all she could to stop Vince. "Were you the one who shot at us?"

"No more talking." He pulled out a gun. "It's time to go."

• • •

Piers had taken the time to don a pair of denims, a cotton shirt, and running shoes that he always kept in the back of his car. He snapped a shoulder holster on, checking the gun for ammunition.

Circling high over the dump, Piers spotted a blue van in a valley formed by mountains of trash. Though the dump was not used anymore, it hadn't all been covered or plowed down. Avenues had been made through the piles of rotting garbage. Would Vince have her near the van? Or would she be somewhere else? There was a damned lot of space to cover.

Arching over and away from the dump, Piers took his bearings, sighted on where the van would be from his vantage point on the ground, and landed the vehicle. A gun in his hand, he was out of the 'copter and running before the blades stopped spinning.

Vince heard the chopper as he untied Damiene's feet. Holding onto her arm, he pushed her out of the van, then looked around. Why was a chopper in the area?

A garbage dump! Damiene thought. That's where she was going to die? Damn Vince Dalrymple. When she felt the gun prod her back, she looked over her shoulder. "Where are we going."

"Not far."

Just far enough to kill her and cover her with trash. Damn the man!

They walked a short distance, turned right, then left along the narrow lanes through the mountains of junk. It was like a maze. And she could hide in a maze.

Glancing sideways to check that Vince was just behind her, she saw him pause to look around. Seizing the chance, she threw her shoulder into his chest, almost unbalancing herself.

He fell to the ground, cursing, and she took off at a run.

Ten

Piers heard the crashing around and sunk down into a gully of trash. Lifting his head cautiously, he edged upward over the mound of junk and looked down on the narrow roadway. Vince! Where was Damiene? Had he killed her? His heart seemed to stop. *Don't think that way.*

Gathering his body for the leap down onto Vince, Piers was so filled with anger, he almost missed the rustling sound to his right.

Pausing for a moment, he listened. Damiene? Pulling back, he edged to one side.

When he saw the fall of silver hair, he almost passed out with relief. She was trying to hide from Vince. The bastard had tied her hands, but still she'd managed to climb up the side of the trash mountain.

Sliding soundlessly down to her side, he clamped his hand over her mouth and smiled into her shocked eyes. "I'm with you, darling," he whispered in her ear. He saw how she struggled to stem the flood of tears in her eyes, and she pushed her face into his shoulder to mask any sound.

"Piers, please," she whispered. "He has a gun. Untie me."

Reaching around her, he wrestled with the knots at her wrist, feeling the welts from the tightly tied rope. Vince would answer for that too.

"Stay here." When she shook her head, he knew there was no arguing with her, that she wouldn't hide when he went to face Vince. "I'll worry."

"Don't. I'll be fine." She watched a smile tilt one corner of his mouth, then he nodded.

He peered down at Vince again. Gun in his hand, Vince was walking slowly forward, looking to the left and right, turning toward Piers, then away. . . .

Piers leapt down onto him, setting off an avalanche of trash. Hearing the sound, Vince wheeled and brought up his gun. He fired and missed. Piers hit him squarely in the chest, and the two men tumbled to the ground. Damiene screamed when she saw Vince roll over on top of Piers, lifting his gun to shoot him. But Piers smashed him in the face, throwing him off. Leaping to his feet, Piers whirled, his gun aimed.

"Give it up, Vince."

"I'll kill you, you bastard."

Vince recklessly threw himself at Piers, knocking him off balance. Damiene half ran, half slid down the mound of garbage, desperate to help Piers. The men were struggling, then Vince wrestled Piers's gun from him.

"Good-bye, *friend*," he sneered.

Damiene hurled herself at Vince, throwing him to the ground.

"Damiene!" Piers yelled. He planted his foot on Vince's hand, forcing him to let go of the gun.

"It's over, Vince," he said bleakly.

"Looks like you didn't even need the cavalry," a voice behind them said.

Piers and Damiene whirled to see Dolph, Bear, and two uniformed policemen standing there.

Dolph wrinkled his nose in distaste. "What a remarkably pretty spot you picked, chum."

"Not my choosing," Piers muttered.

He turned to Damiene, and she flung herself into his arms, fighting to control the sobs that rose up in her. "Are you all right?"

"That should be my question," he said, a tremor in his voice. "Did he hurt you?"

"No." She pulled back and looked down at Vince. "He knew my brother."

Piers nodded. "We figured that."

She stared at him. "How long have you known about Vince?"

"A detective hired by Dolph connected Rustam Dever with some of our problems. We questioned him and got some answers." Piers looked at Vince. "He killed Berto and your brother."

"Take your lady out of here, Piers. We'll handle this," Dolph said. "The police will keep Vince and Dever occupied for some time."

Damiene shivered and pressed closer to Piers. "He lied about my parents. They're not in a hospital."

"I know. I've talked to them and they're fine." He looked at his two friends. "Thanks."

Bear nodded. "Go on. Get out of here."

His arm around her, Piers led Damiene away.

"I think a shower is the first order of business when we get home," Piers said as they drove away from the airfield.

Damiene nodded, watching him warily. He was still wound tight as a coiled spring. She'd never seen this side of Piers Larraby. If he'd had to, he would have killed Vince.

She shivered. So would she.

Piers saw her shiver and reached over to take her hand. She squeezed his gratefully, knowing there would be time later to talk about Vince and Berto and Gilbert. For now it was enough that she and Piers were together.

He lifted her hand and kissed her palm. "What do you say you call your folks and get their blessing?"

"Blessing? For what?"

"For our marriage. I want to marry at once. What do you want?"

"It's crazy . . . but it's what I want too." Damiene laughed. "I'm happy . . . and I'm glad that I can tell my parents that it's really over, that the man who killed Gilbert has been caught."

Piers's smile died. "And I intend to see that the charges stick."

"So much heartache," she murmured.

"But it's all behind us. Right now I'd like to plan a wedding."

"Yes." Damiene hitched as close as she could to him with the console between them. They'd known each other only a matter of weeks. Yet she was ready to give her heart and life to a man who reminded her of an iceberg. Nine tenths of Piers Larraby was under the surface. There was much she didn't know about him. She did know she loved him.

The rest would come in time. She squeezed his hand.

"Yes, Mother, I know it's sudden, but Piers said we'll stop in Rochester after we come back from the Caribbean. Yes, we're going there for our honeymoon."

She turned when Piers tapped her on the shoulder. "Let me talk to her," he said. She handed him the phone. "Mrs. Belson, I've arranged a flight out here for you and your husband so that you can attend our wedding. We're being married by a friend of mine who manages a haven for the homeless here in Las Vegas." Piers leaned down and kissed an open-mouthed Damiene. "I love your daughter and want to make her happy. I look forward to meeting both of you." He gave the receiver back to Damiene.

Still staring at him, she said into the phone, "Yes, he is generous, Mother. I can't wait to see you and Dad." She hung up the phone and turned to Piers. "Thank you. That was kind . . . but it'll be expensive."

"An advance wedding present."

"I thought that was our trip to Key Island in the Bahamas."

"Isn't it allowed to have more than one?" He saw the crease of concern on her face. "Don't worry. I can afford it."

She looked after him as he walked away. Just how wealthy was he?

• • •

The wedding day dawned bright and desert-clear.

Damiene listened to her happily chattering mother, determined not to let her see her sudden attack of the jitters.

"And can you believe a private jet? Oh, Damiene, it was so beautiful. It had a bar and cooking area and the attendant made us all manner of delicious things. Your father napped in a real bed. Such luxury." Her mother clapped her hands. "I don't think you'd ever mentioned that Piers Larraby was rich."

'No, I guess I forgot to mention that."

"Oh, my dear, you look beautiful. That champagne silk makes your skin glow. And I love the empire look, that pencil-thin skirt, the puffy sleeves. You look like an angel."

"Thank you, Mother."

"But you're a little pale. Are you still bothered about what we heard about Gilbert?" Her mother squeezed Damiene's hand.

"Yes, I suppose it will always gall me that he had to die because drug dealers were protecting themselves."

Her mother gazed intently at her. "Are you happy with Piers, Damiene? We want you to be happy."

"I'm happy, Mother."

"Your father was very impressed with Piers and his friends."

"He's a fine man." And he was. So why had several hundred butterflies just taken flight in her stomach?

There was a knock on the door. "Come in," Damiene called.

Bear put his head around the door, grinning. "Piers wanted to come and get you, but we wouldn't let him. It's time to leave for the chapel. I'm riding with you and your parents."

"Thank you, Bear." Damiene smiled at the man who'd become her friend. And if Dolph held himself remote from most persons, he'd shown Damiene affection and respect.

She adjusted the corona of orange blossoms on her head and walked toward Bear.

"You're beautiful, Damiene," he told her softly. "My chum is a lucky man. Trust him, Damiene. You can, you know."

As though sunshine had just poured into her soul, she smiled. "I know that. And I do love him." Doubts filtered away. She and Piers would belong to each other that day. "Let's hurry."

Her mother and Bear laughed.

In the limousine Piers had arranged for them, she sat beside her father and held his hand. "I'm glad you're giving me away, Daddy."

"So am I. Wouldn't Gilbert have loved this?" He touched her cheek. "Don't worry. We're dealing with it, Damiene. We loved him and will always miss him. We know what happened and that's always so much better than conjecture."

"Yes, it is." She squeezed her father's hand.

As they entered the chapel, Damiene's gaze fixed on Piers. He was dressed in a beautifully tailored black suit, white shirt, and discreet burgundy tie. He was magnificient, and she didn't look away from him throughout the entire brief ceremony.

When Piers lifted her chin for his kiss, his knees almost buckled at the brilliance of her smile. He hesitated before kissing her, and she cupped his face and planted her lips on his, kissing him long and hard.

"Lord," Dolph said softly. "Since meeting the beauteous Miss Belson, I can see that I've missed something on this planet."

"I agree," Bear murmured.

They were in the air, in the private jet, winging toward the tiny, private island of Key in the Bahamas.

"It was a wonderful wedding," Damiene said, her eyes half closed as she leaned back against her husband.

"Yes," Piers murmured, his lips pressed to her forehead. "Damiene Belson Larraby. I like that. Sounds imposing."

She smiled. "Sounds good. My mother was right. This is a comfortable plane." Her eyes opened slowly. "And you own it, don't you?"

He nodded. "I haven't been entirely honest with you. I told you that I own several casinos, but that's actually the smaller part of my corporation now. When the casinos began bringing in big money, Berto and I diversified, investing in different companies was well as buying property. Real estate has become my gold mine. I'm really not just a gambler."

She laughed. "I knew *that*, silly. And now I know what you do when you lock yourself in your study every morning. You're running a profitable business." She grinned at him impishly. "And here I thought you were just trying to come up with a system to break the bank playing blackjack."

"Scamp," he murmured, lightly biting her neck.

She laughed again. "And while you were making

money, Dolph was making it on the stage, and Bear was racing." Her husband's crooked smile made her heart beat rapidly. "What a trio!"

"Something like that. Only they do come from wealthy families. But neither is interested in living an idle high-society life. Dolph is an American, but on his mother's side he's related to an English peerage. Bear's family is an automobile empire."

Damiene's brows rose. "He's related to *those* Kenmores?"

"Yes. Now you know all the secrets."

When they reached St. Thomas, they took a helicopter to a small island with a beautiful half-moon bay and white beaches.

"It does look like a key from the air," Damiene said as she and Piers waved good-bye to the helicopter pilot. "Who else is on the island?"

"No one. We're alone. We'll do our cooking and our picking up. Contact with the outside world is by radio."

"If you expect me to protest, think again." She grinned at him. "I've been wanting to get you alone for days." The palpable relief on his face made her chuckle. "I love you. I thought you knew that."

"A part of me did," he said in a low voice. "But a big part of me can't take anything with you for granted. You're a precious gift, one I never hoped to have. I'll always be grateful."

"You know that already, and we've been married only a day?"

"I knew that the first night when we dove behind the cacti."

She reached up and caressed his cheek. "Our lives have been like a Steven Spielberg movie."

"Something like that." He unbuttoned her new silk blouse and pushed it off her shoulders, then removed her skirt and underthings.

"Not worried about low-flying planes?" she asked, her voice husky with arousal.

"Off the beaten track," Piers said hoarsely, yanking his own clothes off.

She looked him up and down, enjoying herself. "You're ready to make love."

"Yes. How about you?"

"Yes, yes, yes." Then she turned and ran for the sea.

Her nude body glistened golden in the light of the setting sun, her silver hair a gleaming contrast. "I'm coming, goddess," Piers murmured, and sprinted after her.

Like children they cavorted in the sea, splashing, diving, swimming.

Then Piers scooped her up in his arms and carried her to the beach, kissing her gently over and over again.

"I like this," Damiene said, twining her arms around his neck. "I haven't been so carefree in ages . . . if I ever was."

"We're perfect together," Piers murmured.

As he carried her along a winding path lined with frangipani and jasmine, she sniffed delightedly. "Umm, what perfumed air."

"Wonderful, isn't it." He was pleased when she gasped at the sight of the one-story bungalow with the wraparound lanai.

Carrying her into the master suite, he let her slip down his body.

"It's beautiful, so—" Damiene began. When her

husband stopped her words with his mouth, she forgot what she was going to say.

In slow wonder he moved down her body. His lips caressed her skin lovingly. No curve or aperture escaped his loving attention.

Heat built in Damiene like a lava flood, and words disappeared into groans of happy ecstasy. Embraces tightened.

Piers felt his whole being tremble as her pliant body undulated under his touch.

Pushing her gently back to the bed, his hands still stroking her, he entered her, taking her and giving himself.

The hot wind of passion whirled them into the rapturous vortex where only lovers could go. Damiene cried out when she felt her body fly apart and join his. Her husky vows of love were murmured over and over again.

"I love you, Damiene, my wife."

"And I love you, Quicksilver. You've saved my life, you've changed my life. Nothing will ever be the same again because I'm yours. You make me so happy."

"That was my intention," he said, kissing her once more.

"Lucky me," she whispered.

"Me too."

THE EDITOR'S CORNER

We've selected six LOVESWEPTs for next month that we feel sure will add to your joy and excitement as you rush into the holiday season.

The marvelously witty Billie Green leads off next month with a real sizzler, **BAD FOR EACH OTHER,** LOVESWEPT #372. Just picture yourself as lovely auburn-haired journalist Keely Durant. And imagine that your boss assigns you to interview an unbelievably attractive actor-musician, a man who makes millions of women swoon, Dylan Tate. Sounds fascinating, doesn't it? So why would the news of this assignment leave Keely on the verge of a collapse? Because five years before she and Dylan had been madly, wildly attracted to each other and had shared a white-hot love affair. Now, at their first reunion, the embers of passion glow and are quickly fanned to blazing flames, fed by sweet longing. But the haunting question remains: Is this glorious couple doomed to relive their past?

Please give a big and rousing welcome to brand-new author Joyce Anglin and her first LOVESWEPT #373, **FEELING THE FLAME**—a romance that delivers all its title promises! Joyce's hero, Mr. Tall, Dark, and Mysterious, was as charming to gorgeous Jordan Donner as he was thrilling to look at. He was also humorous. He was also supremely sexy. And, as it turned out, his name was Nicholas Estevis, and he was Jordan's new boss. Initially, she could manage to ignore his attractiveness, while vowing never to mix business with pleasure. But soon Nick shattered her defenses, claiming her body and soul. Passionate and apparently caring as he was, Jordan still suspected that love was a word only she used about their relationship. Would she ever hear him say the cherished word to her?

Sandra Chastain, that lovely lady from the land of moonlight and magnolias, seems to live and breathe
(continued)

romance. Next, in LOVESWEPT #374, **PENT-HOUSE SUITE,** Sandra is at her romantic Southern best creating two memorable lovers. At first they seem to be worlds apart in temperament. Kate Weston is a feisty gal who has vowed to fill her life with adventure upon adventure and never to stay put in one place for long. Max Sorrenson, a hunk with a bad-boy grin, has built a world for himself that is more safe than thrilling. When Kate and Max fall in love despite themselves, they make fireworks . . . while discovering that building a bridge to link their lives may be the greatest fun of all.

If ever there was a title that made me want to beg, borrow, or steal a book, it's Patt Bucheister's **ONCE BURNED, TWICE AS HOT,** LOVESWEPT #375. Rhys Jones, a good-looking, smooth operator, comes to exotic Hawaii in search of a mysterious woman. At first he doesn't guess that the strawberry blonde he bumped into is more than temptation in the flesh. She is part of what has brought him all the way from London. But more, the exquisite blonde is Lani . . . and she is as swept away by Rhys as he is by her. She soon learns that Rhys is everything she ever wanted, but will he threaten her happiness by forcing her to leave the world she loves?

Welcome back the handsome hunk who has been the subject of so many of your letters— *Kyle Surprise.* Here he comes in Deborah Smith's **SARA'S SURPRISE,** LOVESWEPT #376. Dr. Sara Scarborough saw that Kyle had gotten through the sophisticated security system that guarded her privacy. And she saw, of course, the terrible scars that he had brought back from their hellish imprisonment in Surador. Sara, too, had brought back wounds, the sort that stay buried inside the heart and mind. Demanding, determined, Kyle is soon close to Sara once more, close as they'd been in

(continued)

the prison. Yet now she has a "surprise" that could leave him breathless . . . just as breathless as the searing, elemental passion they share.

From first meeting—oops, make that impact—the lovers are charmed and charming in Judy Gill's thrilling **GOLDEN SWAN,** LOVESWEPT #377. Heroine B. J. Gray is one lady who is dynamite. Hero Cal Mixall is virile, dashing, and impossibly attracted to B.J. But suddenly, after reacting wildly to Cal's potent kisses, she realizes this is the man she's hated since she was a teenager and he'd laughed at her. Still, B.J. craves the sweet heat of him, even as she fears he'll remember the secret of her past. And Cal fears he has a job that is too tall an order: To convince B.J. to see herself as he sees her, as an alluring beauty. An unforgettable love story!

Do turn the page and enjoy our new feature that accompanies the Editor's Corner, our Fan of the Month. We think you'll enjoy getting acquainted with Patti Herwick.

As always at this season, we send you the same wishes. May your New Year be filled with all the best things in life—the company of good friends and family, peace and prosperity, and, of course, love. Warm wishes from all of us at LOVESWEPT.

Sincerely,

Carolyn Nichols

Carolyn Nichols
Editor
LOVESWEPT
Bantam Books
666 Fifth Avenue
New York, NY 10103

FAN OF THE MONTH

Patti Herwick

I first heard of LOVESWEPTs in a letter from Kay Hooper. We had been corresponding for some time when Kay told me she was going to start writing for Bantam LOVESWEPT. Naturally, since Kay was special—and still is—I was eager for the LOVESWEPTs to be published. I was hooked from then on. I read books for enjoyment. When a book comes complete with humor *and* a good story, I will buy it every time. As far as I'm concerned, LOVESWEPTs haven't ever changed. The outstanding authors that LOVESWEPT has under contract keep giving us readers better and more interesting stories. I am enchanted with the fantasy stories that Iris Johansen writes, the wonderful, happy stories that Joan Elliott Pickart writes, and, of course, Kay Hooper's. I can't say enough about Kay's work. She is a genius, her writing has gotten better and better. Every one of her books leaves me breathless. Sandra Brown is my favorite when it comes to sensual books, and I enjoy Fayrene Preston's books also. The fact that LOVESWEPTs are so innovative—with books like the Delaney series and Cherokee series—is another reason I enjoy reading LOVESWEPTs. I *like* different stories.

Now, as for me, I'm 44 years old, married, and have one grandchild. I think that I've been reading since the cradle! I like historical romances along with the LOVESWEPTs, and I probably read between 30 and 40 books a month. I became the proud owner of my own bookstore mostly because my husband said if I didn't do *something* about all my books, we were going to have to quit renting our upstairs apartment and let the books take over completely! I enjoy meeting other people who like to read, and I encourage my customers to talk about their likes and dislikes in the books. I never go *anywhere* without a book, and this has caused some problems. One time, while floating and reading happily on a swim mat in the water, I floated away. My husband got worried, searched, and when he found me and brought me back, he decided to do something so he wouldn't have the same problem again. Now he puts a soft nylon rope around the inflatable raft and *ties* it to the dock! I can only float 50 feet in any direction, but I can read to my heart's content.

I would like to thank LOVESWEPT for this wonderful honor. To have been asked to be a Fan of the Month is a memory I will treasure forever.

60 Minutes to a Better, More Beautiful You!

Now it's easier than ever to awaken your sensuality, stay slim forever—even make yourself irresistible. With Bantam's bestselling subliminal audio tapes, you're only 60 minutes away from a better, more beautiful you!

__ 45004-2	**Slim Forever**	$8.95
__ 45112-X	**Awaken Your Sensuality**	$7.95
__ 45081-6	**You're Irresistible**	$7.95
__ 45035-2	**Stop Smoking Forever**	$8.95
__ 45130-8	**Develop Your Intuition**	$7.95
__ 45022-0	**Positively Change Your Life**	$8.95
__ 45154-5	**Get What You Want**	$7.95
__ 45041-7	**Stress Free Forever**	$7.95
__ 45106-5	**Get a Good Night's Sleep**	$7.95
__ 45094-8	**Improve Your Concentration**	$7.95
__ 45172-3	**Develop A Perfect Memory**	$8.95

Bantam Books, Dept. LT, 414 East Golf Road, Des Plaines, IL 60016

Please send me the items I have checked above. I am enclosing $_____ (please add $2.00 to cover postage and handling). Send check or money order, no cash or C.O.D.s please. (Tape offer good in USA only.)

Mr/Ms _____

Address _____

City/State _____ Zip _____

LT-12/89

Please allow four to six weeks for delivery.
Prices and availability subject to change without notice.

THE DELANEY DYNASTY

Men and women whose loves an passions are so glorious
it takes many great romance novels by three bestselling
authors to tell their tempestuous stories.

THE SHAMROCK TRINITY

☐ 21975   RAFE, THE MAVERICK
          by Kay Hooper $2.95
☐ 21976   YORK, THE RENEGADE
          by Iris Johansen $2.95
☐ 21977   BURKE, THE KINGPIN
          by Fayrene Preston $2.95

THE DELANEYS OF KILLAROO

☐ 21872   ADELAIDE, THE ENCHANTRESS
          by Kay Hooper $2.75
☐ 21873   MATILDA, THE ADVENTURESS
          by Iris Johansen $2.75
☐ 21874   SYDNEY, THE TEMPTRESS
          by Fayrene Preston $2.75

THE DELANEYS: *The Untamed Years*

☐ 21899   GOLDEN FLAMES *by Kay Hooper* $3.50
☐ 21898   WILD SILVER *by Iris Johansen* $3.50
☐ 21897   COPPER FIRE *by Fayrene Preston* $3.50

Special Offer
Buy a Bantam Book
for only 50¢.

Now you can have Bantam's catalog filled with hundreds of titles plus take advantage of our unique and exciting bonus book offer. A special offer which gives you the opportunity to purchase a Bantam book for only 50¢. Here's how!

By ordering any five books at the regular price per order, you can also choose any other single book listed (up to a $5.95 value) for just 50¢. Some restrictions do apply, but for further details why not send for Bantam's catalog of titles today!

Just send us your name and address and we will send you a catalog!